THE
MERIT
BIRDS

THE
MERIT
BIRDS

KELLEY POWELL

DUNDURN
TORONTO

Editor: Shannon Whibbs
Design: Courtney Horner
Printer: Webcom
Cover Design: Laura Boyle
Cover: © Potowizard | Dreamstime.com, © beakraus | iStockphoto.com

Library and Archives Canada Cataloguing in Publication

Powell, Kelley, author
      The merit birds / Kelley Powell.

Issued in print and electronic formats.

ISBN 978-1-4597-2931-5

      I. Title.

PS8631.O83725M47 2015   jC813'.6   C2014-905048-8   C2014-905049-6

1   2   3   4   5   19   18   17   16   15

  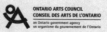

Conseil des Arts du Canada   Canada Council for the Arts   Canada   ONTARIO ARTS COUNCIL CONSEIL DES ARTS DE L'ONTARIO an Ontario government agency un organisme du gouvernement de l'Ontario

We acknowledge the support of the **Canada Council for the Arts** and the **Ontario Arts Council** for our publishing program. We also acknowledge the financial support of the **Government of Canada** through the **Canada Book Fund** and **Livres Canada Books**, and the **Government of Ontario** through the **Ontario Book Publishing Tax Credit** and the **Ontario Media Development Corporation**.

Care has been taken to trace the ownership of copyright material used in this book. The author and the publisher welcome any information enabling them to rectify any references or credits in subsequent editions.
                                                                              J. Kirk Howard, President

Printed and bound in Canada.

The publisher is not responsible for websites or their content unless they are owned by the publisher.

VISIT US AT
Dundurn.com
@dundurnpress
Facebook.com/dundurnpress
Pinterest.com/dundurnpress

Dundurn
3 Church Street, Suite 500
Toronto, Ontario, Canada
M5E 1M2

For my parents, Bert and Paula Powell,
who always said I could

PROLOGUE

He remembered how death had settled so softly onto her body, like the relaxation of a deep breath. He had killed her. It was the only thing he knew for certain. Other than that, nothing seemed real as he nervously crouched in a patch of tall, dry grass. It rustled noisily every time he shifted. He wouldn't be able to stay long.

It seemed to take forever for the slowly moving pickup truck to pass in front of his hiding place. He could see her framed picture on top of the white-and-gold casket that sat on the back of the truck. He felt his throat constrict at the sight of her in the photo, alive and smiling. A tinny death song played from a portable stereo. Her friend, Nana, wept as she led the procession behind the truck; like all of the girls in the procession, she wore a long, white skirt, a flowing white blouse, and a white sash across her heart.

The southeast Asian sun bore down on him; its intensity threatened to drive him out of hiding, but he didn't want to move. Didn't want to leave her again. Sweat trickled down his back. The rusty pickup truck turned into the temple grounds followed by the long line of mourning friends. No family members were there.

Once all of the mourners had safely passed he skulked through the grass, his belly scraping across the hard, thirsty ground, to a thicket of banana trees with wide leaves. From here, he watched as they lifted the coffin onto an enormous pile of broken sticks and branches. He couldn't breathe as Nana lit the match and dropped it onto the pyre. He knelt, hand frozen to his mouth, tears the only thing moving as he watched her body burn. The air became thick with the smoke of death.

Her death.

Nothing would ever be the same again.

BEAUTY AND DEATH

Cam

Eighteen years old and I don't know how to take a crap. The frog mocked me. I knew it. His eyes gleamed in the moonlight as I stood before the toilet, trying to figure out what to do. There was nothing but a hole in the ground with foot grips on either side. The frog croaked out a chuckle when he saw me scan the closet-like bathroom for toilet paper. Only a hose with a sprayer hung from the wall. What the hell was that for?

"Idiot," the frog seemed to croak.

"You okay in there, Cameron?" asked Julia, a.k.a. my mom. I hated her at that moment. It had been her idea to give up everything for a year — her job, our house in Ottawa, my last year of high school, the basketball team — to come here, to Laos. Who the hell goes to Laos? I didn't even know how to say it right. Was it *Louse*, like lice that feed off little kids' blood? Or *Lay-os*, like some weird basketball move? The guy next door — I think his name is Somchai — said, "Welcome to *Lao*." At least he could speak English, and he looked my age, although it was hard to tell.

In this country even grandpas look young. I stomped my foot at the frog and he leapt off to go tell his friends about the freaky foreigner who didn't know how to shit.

This was supposed to be my year. I'd be the best player on the school team for sure. I planned to check out universities, apply for basketball scholarships, go to some good parties, meet girls. Instead my mother had her mid-life crisis and applied for an overseas placement. She left her cushy international development job with the feds in Ottawa for a posting in the sun-scorched capital city of Laos, called Vientiane, where red dust clung to my nose hairs and the stink of fermenting fish filled the air.

We'd arrived just after New Year's. First it was happy new millennium — then it was welcome to the Dark Ages. On the Lao Airlines flight from Bangkok to Vientiane the rickety plane spewed thick smoke into the cabin. Some other foreigners on board freaked out until we realized it was just the air-conditioning malfunctioning. Still, I think the plane must have been a leftover from the Vietnam war.

Stepping off the plane, I immediately realized how bored I was going to be in this country. Everything seemed to be in slow motion. No one hurried to do anything — not even the guys shuffling their flip-flops along the tarmac as they removed our luggage from the bowels of the old plane. Everyone seemed to be either really relaxed, super sleepy, or so high they couldn't move. I couldn't tell which. It didn't take me long to figure out that the heat had something to do with it. I felt like I was in a sauna. The sun seared my eyeballs as we waited for a wobbly three-wheeled taxi called a *tuk-tuk* to take us to the house Julia's department had rented for us.

"Don't complain about the heat yet," Julia said. "It's still the cool season."

During the drive I saw that Vientiane wasn't even a city. It was just a bunch of grubby villages that grew into one another. Oversized jeeps and vans with the logos of international development organizations muscled past us. Guys my age drove past on rusted bicycles with big, girly banana seats. Red dust stuck to the sweat marks on my white T-shirt. I *had* to find a way to get back home.

"Isn't this exciting?" Julia squeezed my hand. It was the first time she had touched me in a long while. Maybe something good would come of this. Maybe she wouldn't be so busy here. I was embarrassed by my babyish thoughts.

"Yeah, great," I said. My response sounded sarcastic, though I didn't mean it to be.

From the glassless windows of our bright blue-and-red *tuk-tuk* I saw bald monks in carrot-coloured robes carrying black, oversized umbrellas to protect them from the vicious sun. A family of four balanced on one motorbike drove past us. We wobbled past skinny palm trees, farmers with triangular hats bent over green rice paddies, and stagnant ponds suffocating with massive lily pads and pink lotus flowers. The smell of diesel made me want to cough and I could feel dust, gritty and coarse, in my mouth. My head was foggy from jet lag and my stomach knotted with resentment.

From my peripheral vision I noticed a woman on the side of the road, crouched over a tree stump. The *tuk-tuk* stopped at a crowded intersection and I saw that with one hand she was holding down a squawking chicken, its scrawny neck bared along the smooth top of the stump. In the other hand she held a knife high in the air, the ferocious sunlight glinted off its blade. She looked dressed up, in a sexy tight top with a high Chinese collar and a long, thin skirt hugging her hips. She looked so graceful in the thick sea of grubby children and rundown wooden shops that lined the roadside. Suddenly, she powerfully brought down the knife. I caught my breath as brilliant red blood sprayed from the chicken's neck and bubbled onto the dusty ground. The chicken's headless body jerked and flapped as it fought death. A band of little kids walked by and barely even looked. I guess fatality was nothing new to them. They seemed more interested in the packages of cakes and cookies that dangled from strings hanging along a shop's entrance. The beautiful woman wiped her shiny brow with the back of the hand that still clutched the long blade. The traffic light turned green and our *tuk-tuk* began to trundle on. I turned around to watch her disappear in the distance, shocked at how beauty and death could get so mixed up together.

We pulled up in front of a faded orange fence and Julia laughed as she tried to figure out how many bills worth of *kip* to pay the *tuk-tuk* driver. I gazed around this strange place where my mother expected me to live.

"This is it, Cam," she said. "Home."

"You think I'm staying here?"

I didn't want to play the part of the typical grumpy teenager. I knew how excited she was. But come on. This was too much to ask. I eyed the red dirt road that snaked through the village. Along it sat a muddled-up mess of houses: wooden shacks sitting on stilts so the breeze could flow underneath, pretentious mansions with wrought iron fences nearly as tall as the houses they were meant to protect, and smaller, cement houses with peeling paint. Our rented house was like one of these: simple and concrete with white paint, burgundy wooden shutters, and a corrugated-steel roof. The kitchen and bathroom were in small, separate buildings behind it; a high fence enclosed the small compound, and bushy trees and plants ran along its outside edges. Inside, there was no grass, only lifeless concrete.

"It's to keep the malarial mosquitoes away," Julia explained.

The property looked like a comatose, concrete island desperately trying to keep the dirty, teeming, chicken-clucking, rooster-crowing life of the neighbourhood out. There were even brown, green, and clear pieces of sharp, broken glass cemented to the top of the fence.

"They say it's a really safe neighbourhood," Julia said when she saw me eyeing the shards.

That evening our rumbling stomachs gave us the courage we needed to venture out of our heavy, wooden front door and into the neighbourhood. A crowd had gathered on the road in front of our house. Men riding home from work on tarnished bicycles stopped to peer through our front gate at the strange newcomers. They waved over schoolchildren, who wore uniforms of crisp white button-up shirts and pleated navy-blue shorts or skirts. The little girls clapped hands over their mouths and giggled into their palms. Julia waved awkwardly. I nodded and looked down at the ground as I followed my mother to the neighbourhood *pho* shop. Thankfully it wasn't far from our house.

The children followed us to the *pho* shop and laughed as we pointed to what we wanted — big steaming bowls of rice noodles swimming in clear broth with green stuff and hunks of meat floating in it. I kept my head down and slurped the noodles as quickly as I could. I was so hungry I was able ignore the unidentifiable, gelatinous beige balls of goop bobbing at the surface. Twenty-one hours on planes and three days of stopovers and sitting in airports had made me too exhausted to care. We had flown from Ottawa to Toronto, Toronto to Los Angeles, Los Angeles to Seoul, Seoul to Bangkok, Bangkok to Vientiane. Julia said the indirect route would save her department a ton of cash.

"Money first," I had scoffed.

From the corner of my eye I could see a small schoolgirl timidly waving her hand to catch my attention. I was too tired to make eye contact and fake that I was nice. I couldn't think of anyone but myself right now. It was dinnertime here in Laos, but back home Jon and the guys would just be waking up.

❧

The next day Julia convinced me to walk with her to the Morning Market. The intense sun penetrated my body like an X-ray in search of something broken. We followed a dirt path along the side of a road. Barefoot vendors pushed large, ramshackle wooden carts filled with green vegetables and tropical fruits I had never tasted before: creepy red, hairy balls called *rambutans* and spiky green jackfruit. The vendors' straw, cone-shaped hats protected them from the unforgiving rays of the sun. I was glad when we finally stepped inside the shade of the market.

I had to follow Julia with my head lowered like a slave so I didn't brush up against the filthy tarps that acted as a makeshift roof for part of the market. The cement floor was slick with liquid; I didn't want to know what it was. Women with babies tied to their backs and hands busy with plastic bags filled with dried rice pressed past us. The stench of raw meat was disgusting. I covered my nose with my hand.

"You look silly," Julia said. I didn't answer. "Come on, I have to buy material for Mrs. Mee — you know that lady who lives next door?"

"Not really."

"I think *meh* means mother. Mother Mee. Anyway, she said she'd make me some *sins*. I'll need them when I start my job."

Sins, the long skirts were called. She was already trying to dress native. She could be so embarrassing. All of the women wore them, only Julia was going to look ridiculous in hers. I knew it. A white woman trying to be someone she wasn't.

"You've got enough sins," I said.

She knew what I was talking about. The story of my childhood: me, alone, while she chased everything else — success, men, money. I hadn't called her *Mom* for years — she never felt like one. I remembered my first day of kindergarten: the bus driver wouldn't let me off because no one was there to meet me after school. We sat on the side of the suburban road, bus door slammed shut, while the bus driver, unable to conceal his irritation, sighed and called the school, barking at the secretary to find out what the hell he should do with me.

Then, as now, Julia ignored me. She grinned stiffly at the Morning Market vendors watching her finger the cotton laid out on tables. She prodded me to greet them in the Lao way, with hands in prayer position and head slightly bowed.

"Say *sabaidee*," she urged. "It means *hello*."

Wanting to please her, sins and all, I mumbled "*Sabaidee*" and a market woman looked at me like I had three heads. Back home I'd been one of the most popular guys at school.

When we got back from the market, Somchai was in front of his house dribbling a basketball. He looked up and threw the ball to me. He pronounced the *a* in my name short, so it sounded like *Cahm*. It means *gold*, he told me. That made me laugh. I thought of all the temper tantrums, all of the fights, all of the counsellors. No one else would call me gold.

I returned his throw, only harder. He grinned and threw it back, just as hard. We spent the next sweat-drenched hour shooting hoops, using a basket tied to a coconut tree. We didn't stop until his mom, Meh Mee, brought us tall, perspiring glasses of sugary lime juice.

"You're good," Somchai said.

"You're not bad, either."

He shrugged. "That's nothing compared to *katoh*."

I was confused about what Somchai meant, but when he went behind his house and returned holding a wicker ball in his long fingers, I realized he was talking about a different kind of game. The rest of the afternoon we volleyed the ball back and forth with our feet. Kind of like hacky sack, only nastier. I left Somchai's house with bruises and scrapes on my shins. I was going to like this guy. Too bad I had to like him and stay in his country at the same time.

CHEESE

Seng

The heat hung heavily on Seng's chubby shoulders, like pails of water weighing down the thin body of a villager. Even children moved slowly and the mangy dogs that crept along the red, dusty road wouldn't eat. Seng wiped his brow with the back of his hand and continued to push his bicycle along, plastic knick-knacks dangling perilously but never seeming to fall from the tall, metal pole he had attached to the back of his bike. Normally, the heat didn't bother him so much — he was Lao after all. But today he was bugged. He kept humming that song all the Americans liked, the one about a Barbie girl. It helped him to forget. He wondered what was so special about girls named Barbara. Or why they were made from plastic. He'd find out once he got to America.

Nothing was supposed to bother him. He was the class clown, the fat guy who was always laughing, the one who didn't take life very seriously. He said *boh penyang* — no worries — more often than most Lao people did, and that was a lot, considering it was virtually the national mantra.

The signs outside of the tourist cafes read *Welcome to Laos! Boh Penyang!* But the truth was he did have worries. Especially when it came to his little sister, Nok. Something was happening at her work and he had his suspicions. He might be stupid, but he wasn't born yesterday.

The fact that Nok had to work because he, Seng, didn't make enough money made it so much worse. With her brains she should be at school.

I am not a failure, he tried to tell himself. *I can do more than make people laugh.*

An array of goods hung heavy like the heat from his Thai-style bike — spoons, forks, little buckets for bathing, matches, a few combs, children's toys. The plastic wares were balanced just right. Not too unstable in case they fell, but not too sturdy, either. He wanted to attract attention. His head looked tiny compared to the massive balloon of brightly coloured plastic that exploded on the pole behind him. As he cycled along he was part salesman, part circus show. No wonder nobody took him seriously.

Usually the Vietnamese sold this kind of stuff, but Seng and Nok were desperate for money. He had bought the cheap objects a month ago from a Chinese salesman, hoping to make some *kip*. He had to sell something today — just one thing. Something to make it all worthwhile.

A group of backpackers, tall, white, and hairy, pointed at him.

"Check out all the stuff balancing on that guy's bike!"

Seng understood their English, or at least those particular words. He liked to think about the big *baci* he would throw if he had 500 *kip* for every time a foreigner said them.

"You like Barbie?" he called out. He knew it made no sense since he didn't actually sell Barbies, but he was okay with that. He wanted to make them laugh. Something about this made him sad, but he wasn't sure why. He should really stop thinking so much. It wasn't good for him. He smiled his wide grin and the *falangs* focused their cameras on his face, deep brown from the sun.

"Cheese!" they said. Seng always thought this was funny because the backpackers usually smelled like cheese, or at least milk or yogurt or some kind of dairy. It was the unmistakable smell of whiteness. Truth was, Seng wanted to smell like cheese. He had tried it once and liked how it filled his belly in a heavy, complete way. It looked so good on those advertisements he saw on Thai television, all melted and creamy. He liked most things he saw on television: microwaves, instant soup mixes, and blonde girls with big boobs. He wanted to go to America someday. He thought about it a lot — walking down the street, free from his plastic merchandise, and on his way to an easy job sitting at a desk in air-conditioning all day long. Biting into a big, fat hamburger with a big, fat white girl beside him. A mind free of thoughts about where to get his next *kip* and most of all, the biggest *baci* at his house that any Lao-American person had ever seen. His oldest sister, Vong, had moved there when she got married. Her Lao-American husband, Chit, had left whatever glitzy American city he lived in to visit Vientiane. He had come to please his aging parents; they wanted him to know his roots, he wanted to know Lao girls. Seng was certain the parents must have been happy when Chit returned with a Lao bride, but

Seng and Nok hadn't seen their sister in a while. Still, he was sure Vong would help him get to the land of cheese, white girls, and big *baci* parties.

"Want to buy?" Seng asked the tourists who had taken his picture. He gestured toward all of the plastic on the back of his bike.

"No, thanks," the tallest one answered.

"So sorry to hear that," Seng said. Then he brightened. "Barbie's plastic, I sell plastic, it's fantastic!" *Use their song*, he thought. *Brilliant marketing plan.*

The tourists laughed. "You really like that song, eh?"

"Most popular song in America," Seng answered proudly. They would not be able to deny that he knew a lot about their culture.

"I've never even heard of that song," one of the girls said.

"It's that cheesy song from a few years ago," another answered. "Guess it takes a while for radio hits to make it to Vientiane." Seng's heart sank. He had to do something to lighten the mood; otherwise, these tourists would never buy anything.

"Cheese!" he suddenly exclaimed. He posed as if someone was going to take his picture again. They all laughed. "So you will buy? Nice comb to brush your chest hair?"

Seng didn't know much about chest hair. Lao guys didn't have it. Surely it would need some grooming?

The group of backpackers exploded into laughter.

"No, thanks, bud," one of the guys laughed and put a hand on Seng's shoulder.

"So sorry to hear that," Seng said, and pushed down on his pedal so he could move away from them. He suddenly felt embarrassed.

He dodged *tuk-tuks* as he pedaled by the Morning Market. Always a showman, he rang his bike's bell for children on their lunch break, their white-and-blue school uniforms overtaking the city's sandy streets like ants on food. They reminded him of his school days. As he and his sisters left for school each morning their mother would slip money into their pockets, her round face filled with pride. Of the three, he was the only one who hadn't lived up to that pride. Nok was always at the top of her class and Vong — well. Vong was in America! What more could be said of her success? But here he was, still trying to make a life for himself.

Girls thought he was too goofy. In school he could make them all laugh, but no one wanted a pudgy clown for a boyfriend. They wanted the smart guys with big muscles. Seng hated schoolwork, especially English. While everybody practised "Have a nice day" and idioms (or was it *idiots*? He never remembered), he sat silent. He felt like an idiom. The only reason he went to English class was to please his mother.

He could remember clearly the day she was taken for political re-education. Even at a young age he had known it was coming. Other employees of King Savang Vatthana had been taken years before, in the months after the communists took the king himself. To this day Seng wondered what his parents had done to keep the communists away from their door for so long. He remembered the heavy, rainy season sky on the day his mother and father were stolen in Luang Prabang, the town where he was born. Lush mountains shrouded in mist. A banging on the door. The greenish beige of the communist officer's uniform. The smell of the cigarette smoke he blew in Pa's face. The peaceful sound of the gong vibrating down from the mountaintop temple, in stark contrast with the chaos that was happening in the town beneath. Luang Prabang, home of the royal family and countless golden temple roofs stretching up to the cool, northern sky, faced the communists' irritation more than other Lao towns. Communists aren't big fans of royalty or religion, and Luang Prabang had plenty of both.

"Take care of each other," Meh had said, her smile doing nothing to hide her fear. "Your father and I will be back."

Seng had been five years old. He never saw them again. Every once in a while he would think he spotted his mother in the crowds at the boat festival, or crouched along the side of the road at dawn, offering alms to monks wrapped in orange robes. He remembered how she liked to put a bit of sticky rice in the monks' bowls. Sometimes a banana or some *kip*. Of course it was never his mother whom he spotted, but it didn't stop him from imagining how it might be to meet her once more. She would take him into her arms and sniff his cheek the way Lao parents did to show affection. After the shock of meeting again wore off, her questions would come. "What have you made of your life, son?" And he would have nothing to answer.

Nothing.

Seng rode his bike home slowly. He hadn't sold a single thing. From the road he could hear Nok in the front yard, sifting rice. She looked so serious.

"Good day at work?" he asked. She nodded without looking at him; she was preoccupied and he was glad. She wouldn't ask him about his sales for the day.

"Don't worry, little sister. Someday I'll take you to America. You won't have to work so hard, and you can go to any university you want."

He knew what her wistful little smile meant. She thought he was a goof like everyone else.

"No, seriously. Vong will bring us there someday."

"Did you write her the e-mail you said you were going to?" Nok asked. He thought he could see something different in her eyes. A heaviness. Her job was definitely getting to her — but why?

"Seng, you're not listening." Nok drew him out of his thoughts. Nothing about the girl was phony, not even her words, although sometimes Seng wished they were. She had a way of making her sentences as direct as an arrow. He, on the other hand, had no problem with phoniness. He hadn't written a letter since high school, but would never admit that he didn't know how to write one. Especially one that was going to be sent to America. On a computer.

"I could write it in English if you want." Nok had aced high school, and could have gone to Dong Dok, Laos's only university. But when she'd graduated there had been no money; she had taken a course on traditional Lao massage instead.

"If I want to write a letter, I'll write one," Seng said and shrugged. He was supposed to be the older sibling after all. He didn't need his little sister taking care of him all the time. "I'll make it there someday," he promised, "and once I do I'll send for you and we'll be living the easy life together. Maybe you'll even find a rich, American boyfriend."

She rolled her eyes playfully and he laughed. She didn't think much about boyfriends and Seng thought that was bizarre, given how many times Lao people ask if you're married. It was a common greeting, like "Where are you going?" or *"Boh penyang."* It was one of those things people just said without thinking. Seng guessed Americans didn't say words just to say them. They were too smart for that.

GHOST EYES

Nok

Nok led her next client into the dim room, the familiar smell of menthol and camphor at her nose. Usually her clients were not that interested in her — only in her services. But this one watched her intently. She showed him to a mattress on the floor and drew a curtain around him. When she returned he was sitting up, wearing the pajamas the house provided with FA NGUM MASSAGE stitched on the chest pocket. She motioned for him to lie down and he nodded with a grin. As she began to work on him she wondered where he was from — England, America, Australia. They were all in Vientiane now.

The *falang* kept his eyes open. Her clients didn't often look at her. When she snapped a toe joint his face winced.

"Your toe hurts?" she asked.

He nodded and sat up.

"You speak English?" he asked, obviously surprised.

She nodded.

"You must be well educated for someone in your —" he paused, searching for the right word "— profession, I guess I'll call it."

"It *is* a profession," she said bluntly. "And a tradition."

He said he was a development worker from France, an employee with one of the international non-governmental organizations that dotted Vientiane. The government had permitted international NGOs — not local ones — to come back to Laos in the early nineties, and since then Vientiane had changed. Signs were painted in English and restaurants selling pizza, sandwiches, and French fries poked their heads from Vientiane's fertile soil, like the frog that always startled her when he popped his head out of her shower drain — uninvited, yet somewhat amusing once she became accustomed to him. Her clientele changed from tired Vientiane workers to chubby foreigners with big noses and blue veins showing through their thin, white skin. To Nok, development meant more foreign food and more clientele.

The Frenchman told her he'd just moved to Laos after years of working for a NGO in Thailand. He quizzed Nok about Vientiane: where was the best hospital? Where could he go for a good beer? She was proud of her country and had fun answering his questions. As his hour gradually expired, his grin grew wider. She thought it was weird, but she politely returned his smile and finished her work on his back before moving onto massaging his head. His pale eyes examined her. She smiled inside as she remembered her sister, Vong, telling her that if she were naughty, a *falang* with empty, blue eyes would eat her.

"Is there a place in here that's more private?" he asked. She was annoyed by the interruption; her memories of her sister were becoming more distant.

"No, why?"

The *falang* chuckled, "I guess I'm used to the more private spaces they have in Thailand."

Foreigners were strange. They wanted more privacy for something that she used to do openly with Vong — first thing in the morning when bones were stiff, or as they waited for the rice to cook after a long day of work. But at the same time foreigners walked through Vientiane streets with tiny skirts or no shirts covering their hairy chests.

"I guess any place is good for it," the foreigner said.

She always massaged Vong inside their tiny house. They would joke and eat spicy papaya salad with their fingers afterward. Nok ached for that.

The foreigner disturbed her memories again — this time by the words of his body. She could sense that he was uncomfortable about something so she smiled to relax him. But with a sudden jerk, the foreigner's soggy mouth was on hers. He forcefully grabbed at her breasts. She could smell his musky body odour and taste the beer he had drunk on her mouth. Her stomach lurched. She screamed and pushed him away, but he lunged toward her again. He was short but thick, with strong, broad shoulders. She hated how scared she was and how powerless she felt. Would he do the same thing in his own country? Her heart boomed with a mix of rage and fear as she heaved him off her again. A salty taste rose in her mouth. Her entire body trembled.

"You bitch!" he spat. "I thought —" He scrambled for his clothes. Nok stared into his pale, empty eyes, and needed to throw up.

BAD SPIRITS OUT, GOOD SPIRITS IN

Cam

I stayed inside the rented house for the next two days. I told Julia it was so I could catch up on sleep and get my laptop set up. This excuse seemed to make her feel better about leaving me alone in the strange house while she visited her new office. The truth was I didn't want to go outside. Nothing out there made sense to me, and everyone stared at me. It was creepy. I tried to sleep, but I couldn't. It's a myth that roosters only crow in the morning. There seemed to be more of the annoying birds than people in this village. Plus my mind would race whenever I lay down. Had Julia told my father we were here?

I was anxious to call Jon back home. Maybe he'd be able to tell me something about Marissa. She was the pretty girl with the locker beside mine. We had started to get friendly last semester, sitting beside each other in chemistry class and using the pretext of helping each other with homework so we could flirt. She had these cute blonde curls, although I think the blonde probably came from a bottle, and she wore purple eye shadow that sparkled under our school's fluorescent lights. We made out at her friend's Christmas party. Then Julia spirited me away to this shithole.

After two days of trying to set up an Internet account and cursing the village roosters, I started at Kaysone International School. I was glad when Julia offered to take me on my first day. She asked her department's driver to take us in his yellow Russian Lada. When he pulled up in front of the school, a low and long building with ceiling-less hallways open to the hot sky, I pretended not to be nervous. The school was built in a horseshoe shape that surrounded a playground for the younger kids and a basketball court. Seeing the familiar, gleaming floors of the court made me feel better. Julia and I walked together to the principal's office. He looked only at her as he spoke.

"At Kaysone International School we have some of the finest teachers from around the world." He eyed my mother's crossed, bare legs as he recited his lines. "Our mission is to challenge, motivate, and grow together." He didn't even seem to notice what he was saying. Apparently, Julia didn't, either. I watched, disgusted, as she nodded absent-mindedly and slyly looked him up and down. Her shiny, brown hair was tied back in a sleek, low ponytail. She wore a tight-fitting *sin* and red high heels.

"Isn't class starting soon?" I interrupted.

"Of course," the principal said. "Mrs. Scott, should you have questions or concerns, please feel free to call or visit any time."

"Please," she said, extending her right hand for a lingering handshake, "call me Julia. I'm Julia White. I haven't gone by the name Mrs. Scott since Cameron's father and I divorced years ago."

The principal clearly brightened at this bit of news. "And where did you say you worked?" he asked.

"At the Canadian development office near Khouvieng Road."

"So you're the new masters of Public Admin they hired. I heard about you. I've got a friend working in that office."

"Word gets around in this town."

"Sure does. Perhaps we could meet for lunch someday?"

"I'm going to go now," I interrupted before I barfed.

Her high heels clicked on the linoleum floor as we walked together toward my homeroom.

"Good luck, Cameron," she said as we paused outside the door. Through the thick glass of the door's window I could see my new classmates eyeing me.

"Thanks," I said. I felt like a kindergartener on the first day of school with her standing beside me like that. Still, I was glad when she quickly reached out her hand and squeezed mine for a split second.

❧

I opened the door and a teacher with a British accent greeted me. He introduced me to my homeroom: English lit. I looked around — a big glass window overlooked the school's soccer field. Everyone sat at wooden desks. It didn't look much different from a classroom at home, except that it was the start of second semester and a ceiling fan hummed instead of a furnace. I was pleased to notice that there were some cute girls. After the period ended, one of them told me her name was Olivia. She was from New Zealand. She asked to look at my timetable and said that we were in the same math class.

"I'll show you where it is," she offered.

"Cool," I said, starting to feel less like an alien.

We walked into math class and she said I could sit at the desk beside her. Other students stole glances as they entered the class, curious about the new guy. The room was noisy with chatter, people talking about what they'd done on the weekend.

"What do you do around here for fun, anyway?" I asked Olivia.

"Go to parties, sometimes downtown. We're planning an overnight trip to Nam Ngum for graduation at the end of this semester. Think your parents would let you go?"

Just then a hush fell over the class as the math teacher walked in, dropping a thick textbook on his large desk at the front of the room with a thud.

"You're Cameron Scott, right?" he said, meeting my eyes.

"Yeah."

A couple students sitting at the front of the room turned to look at me.

"Mr. Scott, we wear uniforms at Kaysone International School. Basketball jerseys are not acceptable, even if they are the Boston Celtics.'"

I hated that I blushed. I had noticed that everyone was wearing white shirts with the school's logo. I looked down and pretended to be searching for something in my backpack so Olivia wouldn't see my red face.

Mr. Rose took the attendance and walked up and down the aisles as he collected everyone's homework. Then he began to introduce the topic for the day — algebra. It was something I was good at.

"Today when we talk numbers we're going to say them in Lao, for practice," he said.

Did the guy think we were in grade one? I looked at Olivia and rolled my eyes.

"Do you have a problem with that, Mr. Scott?"

Damn, he was watching me like a hawk.

"Why would we do that?" I asked, trying not to sound too antagonistic.

"Why not? It's the language of the country we're living in. Don't you think it would be useful to know how to count?"

I hated being talked to like an idiot — I already felt idiotic enough in this country where I understood shit-all. *Who speaks Lao, anyway? No one outside of this puny country.* I felt an acrid taste in my mouth. I knew it well — the flavour of anger. I packed up my books and stood to leave.

"I know all about you, Mr. Scott."

I looked up at Mr. Rose.

"I'm the school basketball coach," he explained in some kind of American accent. "I played college ball with Coach Archambault."

"Oh, that's why." I felt a sense of relief. They knew about my dunks all the way in Laos. Coach Archambault said he talked about me with some of his friends in the international school basketball scene. Kaysone International School knew it was getting a star player long before my feet hit the dusty tarmac of Wattay International Airport.

"Yeah, I've heard about your temper, and I don't want to see it in my classroom."

"Bet you'll like it on the basketball court," I said, picking up my books and walking out, slamming the door shut behind me.

As I stomped down the hallway I thought about what a loser I was. I didn't want to see Olivia again. She probably thought I was a freak. Years of counselling and I still couldn't control myself. But I was so pissed that my old coach back home blabbed about my temper. A few spats on the court, a couple of suspensions, and it follows me halfway around the world? Didn't seem fair. I was lost in thought and didn't notice the little kid sitting just outside the school's gated entrance until I almost tripped over her. The near accident didn't seem to startle her. With big, dark eyes, she looked up at me groggily from underneath a tangle of knotted hair. She held a bag up to me that already had some small *kip* bills in it, and brought a grubby hand to her mouth, as if she was eating something that wasn't there.

I didn't know why she startled me so much. I'd seen beggars in Ottawa before. But they were never little kids, and they didn't look so hungry. I thought of the classrooms I'd just stormed past inside. All of the foreign, ex-pat students and wealthy Lao kids wearing crisp, white school uniforms. She looked so small and sad.

I stepped over her and kept walking.

A million justifications ran through my head. The money would go to some drunken parent for booze, giving would only keep her on the street, what she really needed was food and there was no restaurant around, someone else would give her money and besides, I didn't have any small bills. I tried to explain it away so I wouldn't have to think about her anymore.

I hated Laos.

Back home everything would be so simple. It would be hockey season. I'd be over at Jon's house, texting Marissa while pretending to finish our history homework in the rec room down in his basement. We'd be watching Hockey Night in Canada and mowing down chips and President's Choice cookies. His favourite team was the Canadiens, but I was a faithful Senators fan.

I was making a list in my head of all the food I'd been craving since we got here: frosted flakes with cold milk, steaming poutine, lime popsicles so cold that vapour rose from them when you took them out of the freezer. We didn't even have a freezer here — just a bar fridge that usually only contained take-home containers from the Australian restaurant in town. Julia never cooked.

I was dying to know how the school basketball team was doing this semester. I missed my friends — joking and shoving each other in the change room after ball practice, or messing around on the ski hill with our snowboards. I missed the crisp, clean smell of a frozen winter's day; the tingle on my cheeks when I entered a warm, familiar place after being out in the cold all day long. I even liked Ottawa's wind chills of minus thirty. They re-energized me. Made me feel new. But here in Laos there was no wind chill. There wasn't even wind. The stagnant sauna of outdoors and the lifeless, concrete island that was our house suffocated me. I tore off my Boston Celtics jersey and stood up on my wicker bed, getting as close to the ceiling fan as I could without getting my head chopped off. I was trying to get cool. It seemed to be working until Julia knocked on the door of my room.

"How come you're home so early?" she asked.

"Why didn't you tell me I was supposed to wear a uniform to school?"

"Oh, I didn't know. Gary didn't mention anything about a uniform," she said, as if it was no big deal.

"Who's Gary?"

"The principal."

I groaned. "Yeah, he didn't tell you because he was too busy checking out your legs."

"Hey, our neighbours are having a welcome *baci* for us on Saturday." This was an old technique she had used since I was a kid — trying to distract me by changing the subject. One of the counsellors had recommended it to her to avoid a confrontation.

"I don't even know what the hell that is, but I'm sure you'll like it if there are men you can pick up."

"I don't really know what it is, either," she mumbled and inhaled deeply so she could ignore the part about men. "I think it's some kind of party Meh Mee and Somchai are throwing."

"Whatever it is, I'm not going."

She shrugged, as if she couldn't care less whether we went or not, but I knew it was just an act. She loved this kind of cultural crap.

I was thankful when she finally left, closing the door softly behind her. I looked around my bare room and wondered how I got to be in this place. I had just turned eighteen. Couldn't I have a say about where I wanted to live? The truth was I did have a say, but the choice had frightened me. Before we left Jon's mom had offered me the spare bedroom in their basement.

"You could stay with us for the year that your mom is gone," she had said.

I hadn't even mentioned the option to Julia. Hell, she probably would have encouraged me to do it. Why would she want me in Vientiane, anyway? It's a lot harder to score a boyfriend when your grumpy kid is following you around.

≻

I felt like an idiot having to walk back into Mr. Rose's math class the next day. I wouldn't have gone if he weren't the basketball coach, but I figured if I skipped his class it would hurt my chances of getting on the team. Olivia, the pretty Kiwi girl, gave me a little wave as I walked in. Mr. Rose came in, gave me a nod, and started the lesson. He walked over to me when the other students began independently working out algebra problems at their desks.

"Not the best start," Mr. Rose said quietly, although it felt like the whole class turned to look.

"Guess not," I mumbled, focusing on my work.

"It's not easy getting used to another country and culture." Man, the guy was tall. He loomed over my desk like the CN Tower.

"I don't want to be here," I said.

"Things will get better with time. Look, Cam, I want you on the team. I just don't want you walking in here feeling like it's owed to you."

I nodded.

"We've got a game coming up with a tough Thai team. Based on what your coach back in Canada told me, we need you playing in it. How about you start coming out to practice next week and we'll see what you can do?"

I resisted the urge to smile.

"Okay," I said. Maybe I'd stay in Laos a bit longer. See what the team could do.

"Good." He patted me on the shoulder and practically skimmed his head on the ceiling fan as he returned to the front of the class.

❧

On Saturday morning Julia popped her head in my room. I glanced at the red numbers on the alarm clock on my rattan bedside table and was surprised to see that it was past noon. Finally I had slept in. My brain must be adjusting to the roosters.

"The *baci* party starts at two," Julia said.

"I told you I'm not going," I said and flopped onto my belly, covering my head with a pillow.

"Oh, come on, Cameron. It's for us. Somchai will be there."

Okay, so Somchai seemed kind of cool. We played *katoh* every night, after the sun went to bed and gave us a break from its relentless heat. But still, I wasn't in the pleasing mood today. I didn't want to give her the satisfaction. Back home, when she was feeling really guilty, she'd try to drag me to some stupid event like an art gallery or a jazz festival. When I was very young I was happy to spend time with her, but then I figured out that she did it just so she could show her posh friends that she was a mom who spent time with her kid.

I didn't answer her. Non-committal — just like she had been all these years.

From underneath the cheap, foam pillow I heard the click of my bedroom door closing. Then, through the flimsy wall, I could hear the picking up and putting down of her hairbrush, lipstick, and eye shadow. These sounds always put the butterflies in my stomach. As a little kid, they were a warning signal that Julia was going out, and if Julia went out, a lot of times she didn't come back until I had tucked myself into bed and fallen asleep with the covers over my head — hiding from the creaks and bumps of an empty house.

"Meh Mee said you should wear a collared shirt and long pants," Julia called out through the open space that existed between the mouldy ceiling and the top of the wall that separated our bedrooms. I think the space was meant for air circulation, but it didn't seem to be working. Our house was so stagnant. "I know it'll be hot, but that's the custom."

"Whatever," I mumbled, crawling out of bed. I went outside in my boxers to get air in the small, cemented courtyard. It was rimmed with what Julia called rose apple trees. They were virtually the only things that grew in our little, gated yard. Waving palms and banana leaves were all around the outside, but inside our rusty gates there was no life. Even our backyard was just a flat, cement pad baking in the harsh sun. From what I could tell, poor people's houses weren't like this. They were weathered wooden slats nailed together and surrounded by a pulsating jumble of vines, chickens, and emerald leaves as big as elephant ears. But a yard ruled by Mother Nature, wild and untamed, wouldn't do for the wealthy folks. I guess rich people liked to be in charge. We got lifeless cement — and lots of it. I couldn't breathe.

One singular tree had been strong enough to pierce through a crack in the cement behind our house. It flourished despite the dry season. As I felt the heat of the cement radiating through my bare feet, I could spot Somchai through one of the tree's branches that dared to stretch from our yard to his, braving the multi-coloured shards of glass on top of our fence. He poked his head out of a window with open shutters but no glass or screen. I waved.

"See you this afternoon for your *baci*," he called, flashing an unbelievably wide grin. Why did Lao people always look so happy? Especially the guys like Somchai, who seemed to have nothing. No computer, no stereo, no video games, nothing but a front yard filled with goats and chickens. From what I'd seen, there were plenty of cellphones and SUVs in Vientiane, but not for people like Somchai. Still, he always seemed to be smiling about something.

"Okay," I called back, resigning myself to the inevitable. *I'll suck it up and go because I like this guy. Definitely not for Julia.*

We arrived at around two o'clock, just as Meh Mee had instructed. She met us at the door in a drenched sarong, her long, greying hair dripping on the wooden step out front. She didn't speak much English, so she just looked down at the wet fabric clinging to her plump body, belly-laughed, and pulled the sarong up higher over her huge breasts.

"She just finished her bath," Somchai explained from behind her. I'd be so embarrassed if my mother answered the door this way, but he didn't seem to care.

"I got dressed up for this?" I muttered quietly to Julia as Somchai, who was decked out in long khaki pants and a fancy shirt, seated us on the floor and brought us luke-warm glasses of water. Meh Mee's shabby house consisted of one large room. A mosquito net hung in a corner, hovering over a plastic mat that I guessed was someone's bed. A cabinet filled with plates, dusty, pink plastic flowers, and family photos sat beside a window with rain-beaten shutters and no screen. I could hear chickens clucking and an animal scratching, maybe one of their scruffy dogs digging in the dirt around their house.

Julia had tied her long, brown hair back into a bun at the nape of her pale neck, like the Lao mothers do. She was wearing the *sin* Meh Mee had made for her — a chocolate-milk colour, like the Mekong River that oozed sluggishly through Vientiane. She thought she looked beautiful, I could tell. I thought she looked like she was trying too hard.

We sat by ourselves on Meh Mee's floor for what seemed like an hour. Our hosts had disappeared.

"Great welcome party, Juls," I leaned over and whispered. "This place sucks."

"At least we get to spend some time together," she said.

Her comment surprised me. I didn't know she felt that way. Wasn't I was just an annoyance in her life? I tried not to let her see how good her words made me feel. Suddenly we heard the clattering of dishes from the outbuilding behind the house.

"Well, I've had enough," Julia said, getting up from her polite Lao lady position with legs tucked off to the side. I got up and followed her to the kitchen. I always seemed to be following her. "Let's make up an excuse to leave."

We were surprised to find the little outbuilding jam-packed with people. All this time we thought only Somchai and his mother were in the house, but not one inch of empty space could be seen in the simple kitchen. A small, wooden counter was stacked with food — chillies floating in unrecognizable liquid, massive baskets of sticky rice, various animal parts carved up and put onto plates. The sink was filled with water and leaves of floating lettuce. Everywhere people — mainly women, but a few guys, too — laughed and chatted wildly, as if someone amongst them was a stand-up comedian. One toothless granny stood over the counter rolling spring rolls. Another crouched on her haunches and hacked at a huge green papaya; the thin, unripe shreds fell into a red plastic basin. The heat made my collared shirt stick to my armpits with sweat and the stomach-churning smell of fermented fish was everywhere. When I complained about it, Julia explained that the smell was from *padek*, a kind of fish sauce Lao people eat with everything.

"Can we — can we help?" Julia asked Somchai as he entered the kitchen. She was obviously taken aback by the number of people crammed into the small space.

"No, no, you are our guests. Go back to the main house and rest until the ceremony starts. We're just waiting for the *mawphon* to arrive," Somchai said.

"What's that?" I asked.

"The wish priest who leads the ritual."

His answer didn't exactly clear things up for me. Ritual? Were we sacrificing a sheep or something? I was starting to feel uncomfortable, and not only because I was wearing long pants in the middle of a steam room that stunk like rotting fish.

"I want to help," Julia insisted.

A middle-aged woman slicing tomatoes on the floor waved my mother over. It looked like the woman was about to play a practical joke because the room erupted into laughter as Julia sat on the floor beside her.

Feeling conspicuous, I made a beeline for Somchai. As I crossed the floor I hoped the sweat running down my legs wouldn't make it look like I'd pissed my pants. I was painfully aware of every single eye in the room following me. I stepped over people, trying not to step on anyone's fingers, to where Somchai was tearing lettuce leaves in the corner of the dimly lit room. The floor beneath me creaked as I walked on its wooden boards, soft and swollen with the humidity. Just as I reached my friend I heard an ear-splitting crack. I swivelled my neck and apprehensively looked all around. Maybe this neighbourhood wasn't so safe after all. The floor lurched beneath me. My heartbeat started to quicken. But when I felt my feet land on the earth beneath the makeshift kitchen with a dull thud, I realized the crashing sound hadn't come from a weapon. I caught my breath and looked down at my feet; my torso poked up through a hole in the decaying floorboards so I could still see the crowded room.

It seemed as if every mouth and utensil in the room dropped. There was nothing but silence. Looking like I had pissed my pants was nothing compared to this. *What a goddamn loser*, I thought. *Breaking a poor family's floor*. I felt my face flush and a familiar anger rising up from the pit of my belly. *Breathe, Cam*, I told myself. I looked up at Somchai guiltily. I felt like I had betrayed him somehow, but when our eyes met he burst into laughter. Next thing I knew the entire room was laughing, slapping their hands in their laps and wiping tears of hilarity from their eyes. The laugh-fest continued as Somchai came over and helped me out of the hole.

"I feel like an ass," I told him.

"Then I guess we have an ass-hole in our floor," he said

and started laughing so hard again he couldn't speak. After awhile he said, "Are you okay? I'm so sorry. Our floor is old."

Shouldn't I be the one apologizing? After everyone had crowded around me to make sure I was okay, I huddled in a corner of the kitchen washing endless clumps of cilantro and hoped the shame would wear off. But as party guests arrived I could tell each one was told the story by the way I was pointed at. Somchai, my saviour, handed me a shot glass filled with clear liquid.

"What is it?"

"*Lao lao*. Rice whiskey. Every person here drinks from this same glass. For solidarity."

I didn't see what sharing saliva had to do with solidarity, but I was thankful the liquor was strong enough to kill off germs, and some of my shame.

Soon my mother and I were shepherded back into the main house. A crowd of people had gathered in a circle on the floor around a tall centrepiece made from bright orange-and-yellow flowers.

"Look at all the marigolds!" Julia exclaimed.

"Put your left hand here," Somchai said, touching his long, slender fingers to the bottom of the centrepiece, his palm facing up. "And hold your right hand like this." He held it up like he was going to do a karate chop. Countless brown hands clutched long, white strings tied to the centrepiece. The strings stretched all the way to the back of the room. A man who seemed to be leading the whole thing began chanting. I guessed he was the wish priest Somchai mentioned. I had no idea what he was saying. Sweat dripped down my back, fell off my nose, and stung my eyes. The chanting seemed to go on forever. At first I was embarrassed to be sitting in the middle of the circle, closest to the centrepiece, while the rest of the partygoers sat behind me. But now I was glad they couldn't see me as I counted the number of tiles on the ceiling and daydreamed about which university would offer me the biggest ball scholarship. But the *mawphon* caught me and made eye contact. He bobbed his grey head, smiling gently, as he continued to chant. He wore a button-up shirt and khaki pants. Whatever a wish priest was, he didn't look any different from the other men at the party. When the chanting finally stopped, I searched for the closest exit. I needed some air. But a throng of people blocked my way. They crowded around me and tied countless white strings around my wrist. They kept repeating the same phrase.

"It means bad spirits out, good spirits in," Somchai explained. He hadn't left my side the whole time.

Too bad it didn't work. Bad spirits would follow me everywhere in this country.

BUTT-UGLY CALLUSES

Cam

On the Monday after the *baci* I went to school and half-way through homeroom it felt like someone had my guts in a vice. Clutching my stomach, I made it out onto the street without embarrassing myself in front of the ex-pat girls. But there was the little beggar girl again, sitting in front of the school staring into space. She wore a dirty, pink T-shirt with a picture of a blonde princess on it. It was too small for her and I could see her bloated belly sticking out. It was the same thing she'd been wearing the first time I'd seen her. She looked up when I passed by and I thought maybe she recognized me. She held her hands in a *nop*, or prayer position, and dipped her head to greet me. I walked past, trying not to make eye contact so she wouldn't expect anything from me.

There were so many *tuk-tuks* crawling over Vientiane's roads that a driver was stopping for me before I had time to practise in my head how to say the directions to our house in Lao. I tried to tell the driver where I wanted to go, but he looked at me like I was a freak. By the time he figured out what I was trying to say I thought I was going to shit my pants. I climbed into the back of the *tuk-tuk* and slunk down onto the fake red leather. The driver laughed and chattered on about something. I think he was trying to explain why my words were so funny. Somchai told me that the soft, nasally Lao language is tonal, which means the same word can mean different things depending on your tone. Like *mou* can mean "friend" or "pig," depending on whether the sound comes from your throat or your nose. *See* can mean "will" or "fuck." When Somchai told me that I started counting how many times a day I tried to say "I will."

When we pulled up in front of our faded, orange gate I realized that I didn't have any *kip* on me. There were no debit cards or credit cards here, so it was cash or nothing. I tried to tell the driver I didn't have any money and he could come back later to get some, but he didn't understand. He threw his hands up in the air and waited, although he didn't seem that bothered. I looked up the red dirt road of our neighbourhood, hoping I'd see Julia being driven home from work by the office driver. I felt like I was going to pass out. Finally, I spotted Somchai rounding the corner. He smiled as he rode up to us on his creaky, rusty bike.

"I'll pay you back," I said after I had explained the situation.

"Of course," he said and went into his home, coming out moments later with the cash.

I unlocked our door and ran to the toilet. At least now I knew how to use it. Afterward, I collapsed into the wicker bed Julia had bought at the market. The rusty ceiling fan

creaked irritatingly and sucked at making my room cooler.
I couldn't believe it wasn't even hot season yet. The open
window let the smell of Meh Mee's frangipani bush in. I
heard rats scurrying up in the rafters.

I knew Julia would be gone all day, so I was on my own.
Just me and my Lao stomach bug. I passed out and woke
up to the sound of someone rattling our front gate.

"Drink this," Meh Mee said and handed me a plastic
bag filled with clear liquid.

"What is it?"

"Nam wan."

I had no energy to ask for a definition. I drank the
sweet fluid and stumbled back to my bed.

Next time I woke up dishes were clinking in our
outdoor kitchen. It bugged me that I brightened at the
thought of my mother being home early. When I looked
out of the dusty window above my uncomfortably hard
bed I saw Meh Mee stirring something in a blackened pot
on our stove. I opened my mouth to call out the window
to her, but nothing came out.

Soon Meh Mee was bringing me a bowl of what looked
like porridge made from rice.

"Eat," she said in Lao and waited until I did. We didn't
speak as I slowly ate the bland gruel. She just stood there,
making sure I ate every last gluey bite. When I finished she
took the empty bowl back into the kitchen without a word.
The next time I woke up the sun was gone. I heard a chopping sound and looked out my window to see Somchai high
up in a coconut tree that stretched from his yard over ours.
He hacked madly in the darkness with a shiny machete.
Julia still wasn't home, but I didn't feel lonely.

"What freaky Lao sport is that?" I called out to Somchai. I actually had a voice now.

"Meh told me to get you some coconut water. It's good for the belly."

Somchai shimmied down the tree and slashed open his harvest. He held a young, green coconut up to my cracked lips and I drank noisily.

When Julia came home later that night she felt guilty.

"Honey! Are you okay? You should have called. I told you I've got my cellphone all hooked up now."

"Meh Mee and Somchai took care of me."

"I'm so glad."

"They barely even know me."

"I don't think that matters here." She smoothed my bedsheets.

"They barely even know me and they took care of me."

She sighed. "Yeah, and I'm your mother and I didn't take care of you. That's what you're trying to say, right, Cameron?" She looked annoyed and bored at the same time. "Look, let's not start this again. How about I take you for a Lao massage tomorrow? I tried one the other day and they're amazing. It will make you feel like a million bucks." She was using her distraction technique again.

"I don't like strangers feeling me up."

"Don't be silly, honey. It's part of Lao culture. "

Of course I followed her to the massage house the next day. We climbed out of a *tuk-tuk* in front of an old two-storey French villa with yellow paint peeling from its sides. FA NGUM MASSAGE was the only thing written in English on the homemade wooden sign out front. A family stared at us as they drove past on one rickety bicycle.

The mom sat behind the dad with a preschooler on her lap and both of her legs politely hanging to one side. A baby was balanced on the crossbar. No one wore helmets.

"Foreigner! Foreigner! Big-nosed foreigner!" the little boy laughed as he pointed to me.

I stood a bit closer to Julia. I really didn't want to go inside, but I felt like a geek at a party who didn't have anyone to talk to. I didn't want to hang out by myself. Begrudgingly, I followed her into the massage house. When the girl at the front desk handed us pajamas, I wanted to take off. This was stupid. The girl led us upstairs and pointed for us to put our feet in warm, soapy water. Masseuses knelt by our feet and began to scrub harshly. I could see the muscles in their brown arms flexing as they worked, and was amazed at the strength of their slender bodies. My masseuse's shiny, black hair fell all around and tickled my shin as she bent over my feet to dry them with a rough towel. When she looked up and motioned for me to stand I noticed her silky, cinnamon skin and deer-like eyes. Crap. I was wearing peppermint-striped pajamas that were way too short and I had a hot girl rubbing the butt-ugly calluses on my feet.

I followed the girl's glossy hair into a room with mattresses covering the floor. She motioned for me to lie down and drew a curtain around us. I was worried I was going to get a hard-on and the flimsy pajamas would do nothing to hide me. She knelt at my feet and began to massage them rhythmically, first the soles, then the tops, then around my ankles. I knew by the way she yanked each toe that she wasn't someone to mess with. There was a strength and power to her willowy beauty. Such a turn-on. As she worked, it was as if she was kneading frustration out of me. She worked away at the bitterness built up in my muscles. The rhythm of her movements and the calm music made me feel so relaxed. So this was Lao people's secret to being chilled out all the time. I must have fallen asleep because the next thing I knew she was rocking me awake. She smiled in a way that made me wonder if I had done something embarrassing while I was asleep. I rubbed my face to check for drool. She led me to some couches where Julia was sipping from a teacup. My brain was so blissed out it couldn't think of any Lao words to thank her or ask her name.

"So? Did you enjoy it?" Julia pulled me out of my daze.

"Yeah, I did," I said absent-mindedly, and looked around to see if the girl was still in the room. She was gone.

FALANG

Nok

Nok hunched over the mortar and pestle, grinding healing herbs to use on clients. The smell of the crushed plants reminded her of when she'd had to go to the hospital with dengue fever when she was little. As her temperature shot into the cloudy sky of Vientiane's rainy season, her big sister covered her forehead with cold cloths and brought her bowls of rice porridge. The feeling made her cozy, remembering how Vong had cared for her.

Nok had refused to go to the doctor, because she understood even at a young age that they couldn't afford the fee. But her headaches grew sharper, like glass smashing on a cement floor, and she crouched in a dark corner away from the brightness of the sun and the noise of the village. Vong insisted she see a doctor and convinced the head of their village to help her pay for the cost of the initial visit. She'd ended up lying listless for a week in the hospital. Vong did everything she could to pay for it; she sold spicy papaya salad at a roadside shop all day and worked the night shift at the garment factory sewing T-shirts with Western brand names. During her breaks she would come to the hospital to bring Nok some *kanom* and sweet, warm soy milk.

Now Vong had been gone for three years already. Nok was thirteen when she left, Seng was seventeen. Old enough for a couple of orphans to take care of themselves. Nok was so happy for her sister when she said she was marrying a North American and moving away. All the way across the ocean, she said. Vong's future was set. But Nok hungered for her like she did for their mother. Their family of five had been whittled down to two — just her and Seng.

Her thoughts were broken by the front door of the massage house opening. She overheard a foreigner asking for her and her heart skipped. But it wasn't the foreigner with the pale, mean eyes. He had been in her nightmares every night since the assault. Thankfully, it was the grumpy *falang* in the basketball shirt. The one who had fallen asleep. He was pointing her out to Nana. He seemed harmless enough, but why did he need her to massage him again? She didn't trust white guys now.

Nana looked at her imploringly. They needed the business. Not wanting her friend to lose face, Nok nodded that she would do it. She plunged her capable fingers deeply into the *falang*'s flesh. She worked his long body — pounding the bottoms of his feet, manipulating the muscle of his calves, stretching out the tightness of his legs. With each pinch she released some of the resentment that coursed through her tendons. By the time she reached his face her bitterness had begun to fade. As she massaged his cheekbones she noticed the smattering of freckles across his fine nose. There was something sweet and exotic about them. Lao guys didn't have freckles. When she finished, the foreigner sat up, blinked his eyes, and in bad Lao asked her name. She answered, and in order to be polite asked him his name.

"Do you like doing that?" Cam asked.

Nok thought for a moment. No one had ever asked her that before. She did think a lot about how life would be different if she could've gone to university instead of going to work right away.

"It reminds me of my sister, because I used to massage her in the evenings before we slept. So yes, I guess I like it," she said.

"Hey, your English is good." The *falang* looked happy about this.

"Thanks. I studied a lot."

"I'm new here," he said.

"You all are," Nok answered and stood up to leave.

SHARDS

Cam

"Cam, I'm so glad you're getting into Lao culture," Julia said when my visits to *Fa Ngum Massage* grew more frequent. But Somchai figured it out pretty quickly.

"Meet a beautiful *poosao*?" he asked one evening when I got back from the massage house. I just grinned and passed the basketball to him harder.

I could tell Nana was trying to hide a smile each time I requested Nok to be my masseuse, but I noticed how Nok's body would stiffen when Nana led me to her. Was that a good sign? I didn't think so.

We began to talk about a lot of things after each massage. I asked about her parents and she said they went to political retraining camp. She said it was like a school where the Lao government sends people to learn about communism.

"When are they going to be done?"

Nok just shrugged.

I surprised myself by beginning to talk about my dad. The last time I'd said his name I was seven years old. I'd been waiting all morning for him to pick me up and take me fishing. Kneeling on the couch, my nose pressed against the window, I waited for his car to pull into Julia's driveway.

"Great day for fishing!" she had said brightly as she'd opened the curtains that morning. But she was growing increasingly agitated. I could tell by the spastic way she cleaned the kitchen, folded the laundry, tried to keep busy.

I watched as our neighbour across the street pulled out of her driveway and came back some time later with a trunk full of groceries. I saw Matthew from down the street practising how to ride without training wheels. His dad held on to the back of his bike seat and ran beside him over and over again, just like I'd seen other parents do. Parents except for mine; I still needed training wheels.

My father had called me two weeks earlier and promised this would be the day. We would catch a lake trout big enough for dinner, he said. I hadn't seen him in a year and a half. He was going to be amazed at how tall I'd grown.

"Maybe you should call him?" I said to Julia. "See if he's still coming."

But by this time, Julia's forced cheeriness had fizzled. "I'm not calling that bastard."

I whined at her to call him, but she just went back to her frenetic housework. I tried screaming and she ignored me. I pounded on her chest with clenched, seven-year-old fists. She left the room and I frantically grasped at whatever I could and chucked it until it smashed. A Royal Doulton figurine that was my grandma's. A crystal sugar bowl Julia only used when company came. I liked that I was in charge of how they broke, how I had produced the razor-sharp glass shards myself.

Julia came back into the room but didn't say a word. She had seen these kinds of tantrums before. The counsellor had instructed her not to react when they happened, to stay calm, keep cool. He (or was it she? I had seen so many counsellors by age seven I can't remember) told me to count to ten, take deep breaths, think of something that made me feel good. But he didn't know how good it made me feel to see my mother's cherished belongings smash against her expertly wallpapered wall.

She picked me up, and, with my arms thrashing viciously, carried me into my room. That was before I was stronger than her. Later, she would have to just leave the house. It was the only thing she could do.

In my room I overturned the oak dresser Julia had bought after the divorce. I punched a hole in the wall — the third one in two months. My mother wouldn't even bother repairing it. When I was finished I lay on my bed. Now there was space. Now the deep breaths could come. Now I felt calm. But now my father would definitely not come. He would never come again. Who would want to spend time with an angry kid like me?

I couldn't believe I was telling Nok all this crap. I'd never talked with a girl about stuff like that before. I'd never talked to *anyone* like that before. I liked the way she just seemed to accept everything. She didn't try to make it better, she just listened. There was nothing fake about her. I don't even think she wore makeup.

"Do you want to come to my basketball game tomorrow night? We're playing a team from Thailand. They're supposed to be tough to beat."

"No," she said bluntly.

"Why not?'" I asked, trying not to sound too desperate. She didn't answer.

>

The next night, I was still wondering "why not." I wasn't focused on the game. Also, Julia said she was going to come watch, but hadn't shown up. I kept checking the sidelines for her.

"Cam, where's your mind today? You gotta wake up out there," Mr. Rose said. "We've got to be ready for the tourney in Thailand."

Mr. Rose had figured me out a bit, and knew to back off when it was obvious that I was pissed. I was starting to like how he coached — firm and smart. Our team was getting pretty good. The first time I went to a practice I was disappointed. The team seemed like a pile of barf from different countries, speaking different languages, playing different styles. But we'd started to really come together.

I was trying hard to concentrate when I was fouled by the Thai team's star guard. He'd had it out for me since the beginning of the game. I could tell by the way his intense, dark eyes focused on me. I knew he was trying to distract me. But I wasn't going to let him screw up my game. I had learned a couple things in Laos. Being chilled out had its benefits. Still, the game was getting intense. Tied at forty-three apiece by half time. I soon became lost in it.

It was moments like these that made me love basketball. I loved how it could make me forget. Forget my past, my insecurities, even forget myself. During times like these the only thing I thought about was the game. The only thing I heard was the heavy breathing and grunts of the players around me and the squeak of shoes on the polished court. I was simply me. But when the Thai guard fouled me again, he took me out of that space. I hated him for it, but I told myself to be calm. I scanned the perimeter of the court, but Julia still wasn't there and the game was almost over. The Thai guard started shoving me whenever he was in arm's reach.

"What's your problem?" I asked the next time we were close.

"So you're the hotshot new guard." His breathy voice was thick with adrenaline.

I met his taunting eyes.

"Not much," he said, and spat on the floor.

Breathe, Cam.

Don't let it get to you.

I wondered if the words were mine, or one of my counsellors'. Shit, now my concentration was really broken. Where the hell was Julia, anyway? Maybe with Gary, the principal, again, or maybe her friends from work. Whoever it was, they were obviously more important than me.

Breathe, breathe, breathe.

The play started again and suddenly I was running up the court on a fast break. This was my chance to show what I could do. To live up to my reputation as a star ball player. My heart pumped up in my ears and my endorphins soared. I didn't take my eyes off the hoop. I was just about to take a shot when the Thai jerk tripped me. I landed on the gleaming, wooden floor with a hard thud. My teeth cut into my lip like a little kid who fell while learning to walk.

"Forget it, Cam," Mr. Rose yelled. "Forget it!"

I tried. I lay on the floor counting to ten. Then I counted backwards. Then I even counted in Lao. I thought about what Somchai would do in this situation. He'd somehow find it funny. But through my sweat-stinging eyes I saw the Thai guard hovering over me, laughing.

"I heard you're good at ball and your mother is a whore," he said in between heavy breaths.

My teeth clenched together.

"I know the first part isn't true." He laughed. "Maybe you could give your mother my number and I'll see about the second part."

All of my attempts to keep it together took off like a flock of birds that had just heard the shot of a hunter's gun. I jumped up and grabbed his throat.

"Cam, stop!"

He punched my face. I lunged at him viciously, carelessly, like an animal about to rip open its prey. I heard a girl shriek and saw scarlet red on the floor. I inhaled the metallic smell of fresh blood. Mr. Rose and the ref were grasping at us, desperately trying to pull us apart. But I didn't care. I saw fear in his eyes and I liked it. I was in control of the destruction. I punched his face over and over again. I would let him have it. In my mind, I heard Julia's fragile, crystal sugar bowl smashing and crashing to the floor.

LOVING BROTHER

Seng

Seng remembered the story their mom used to tell them. The one about the pregnant woman sacrificing herself. Meh's eyes would grow wide and her voice would soften to a suspenseful whisper as she described in detail how the woman had flung herself into the deep hole hundreds of years ago, when *Si Muang* temple was being built. Meh wasn't trying to scare them, she was trying to teach them a lesson. About sacrifice. Or was it about the temple and why it was so great? Seng realized that perhaps he hadn't got the lesson. He was sure it was a good one — something that he was supposed to remember his whole life. Nok would know what the lesson was supposed to be. She was always brave when Meh told it; she would laugh as he ran and hid underneath the sleeping mat they shared on the floor. That story always gave him the shivers. Especially the part about the temple pillar being lowered on top of the woman while she was still alive. She sacrificed herself, and her baby, to become city guardian of Vientiane. Her spirit was supposed to bring the temple good luck. If you went to pay her homage and asked an old Buddha image to make your dreams come true they surely would. At least that's how Meh always ended the story. Maybe she only did to make him feel better.

"I saw you coming out of *Si Muang* temple today," Nok said over dinner as she rolled sticky rice in her hand. She smiled knowingly. "Are you dreaming for something to happen?"

"Why?" Seng was embarrassed. He scratched the back of his neck. He didn't want her to know how much he thought about leaving Laos. If he could make it to America, people would know he was someone more than a fat peddler of plastic.

"You must have gone to ask for good luck with something."

"How about your work today?" Seng tried to push the topic of conversation off of him. He didn't want to tell Nok anything until he had good news from Vong. Surely their big sister would come through and help him get to America. It was the least she could do.

"Let's not talk about work. It's over, big brother. Focus on your food. You like the fish?"

Now Nok looked like the one feeling uneasy. She was always that way about her work. *Maybe it's because she shouldn't be working*, thought Seng. With her brains she should be studying. After all, she was still sneaking into sociology lectures at Dong Dok University even though she had been caught and told that only those paying tuition could attend. She should be studying at a good university, like an American one. He'd find a way to make it happen. He'd ask his best friend, Khamdeng, to help him contact their older sister.

61

"Do you think I could send an e-mail to Vong next time you work at your brother's shop?" he asked Khamdeng when they met on the riverbank after dinner. Khamdeng had an older brother who just opened up an Internet café, one of many that sprung from the tourist industry.

Khamdeng laughed as he eyed Seng scratching the back of his neck. "You're excited."

"No, I'm not."

"Yes, you are."

"No, I'm not."

"Yes, you are."

"No I'm not."

"Yes, you are."

"Can we stop now?"

"You always scratch your neck like that when you're excited or nervous about something."

"No, I don't."

"Yes, you do."

"No, I don't! I was just scratching a mosquito." Seng suddenly took his eyes off his friend and let his hand drop from his neck down into his lap. Three foreign girls walked by. Seng couldn't take his eyes off them. One had long, blonde hair shining down her back, sky-blue eyes, and a face as sweet as vanilla *kalem*. She walked slowly, her eyes wide, scanning everything around her — the river, the farmers' wives selling vegetables, the bald monks floating by in their orange robes. She was like a child seeing something for the first time.

He tapped Khamdeng on his chest.

"You help me get to America, brother, and I'll introduce you to a girl like that."

Suddenly, the girl seemed to notice them, crouching along the riverbank. Seng sat up tall. Maybe she would come over and talk to them. He looked at Khamdeng and winked.

His friend laughed.

"Cheese!" Seng called out.

The girl's eyes paused on him for a second, but then went back to their scanning, as if she hadn't heard him. As if he was merely scenery to be observed and not the most handsome man she'd ever seen.

"You don't know anything about girls," Khamdeng said.

"We'll see what you say when I bring my American girl-friend back here to visit. Are you going to help me write the e-mail or what?"

Khamdeng reached over and playfully slapped Seng on the back of the head. "You have to ask? I'm your friend, stupid. Friends don't say no to a request for help."

"But it has to be in English so Vong sees that I would be a great help to have in America."

"Okay, I did pretty well in English class. Better than you, anyway." He threw a pebble into the Mekong. "Do you have an e-mail account?"

"No."

"Okay, no problem. We can use mine."

"Do you know her e-mail address?"

"No."

"You need that. We can't send anything without it."

"So sorry to hear that."

"Do you know how to type?"

"No."

Khamdeng cracked up. "Still the class clown."

Seng laughed, too, even though he didn't find it so funny. He'd never used e-mail before. How was he supposed to know you needed an address?

He remembered Vong had written something about e-mail at the bottom of a card she'd sent last Lao New Year. That night after dinner he asked Nok to see the card again. He brought it to Khamdeng and he had been right — her e-mail address was written at the bottom. *An auspicious sign*, he thought.

It took them hours to craft the first message. When they were finished they sat back in the flimsy, plastic Internet café chairs and high-fived each other. Seng knew Vong would not be able to ignore the brilliance of his message:

> *Dear Vong,*
>
> *I am young brother Seng. Three years ago you marry and you go to America. I want to join with you. Here in Vientiane selling plastic goods all day long nobody buy. No kip. Vietnamese job. Better for me come to you. I cook you nice cheese hamburgers and I invite you to big baci party (at your house). Please help me come to America. I am waiting your answer.*
>
> *Little sister Nok has good health and is still smart but she so serious now like old woman.*
>
> *Loving brother,*
> *Seng*

Seng made Khamdeng check for a message from Vong every day.

"Anything?"

"Not yet."

"So sorry to hear that." Seng looked down at his feet. "Are you sure you sent it?" he looked up hopefully.

"Yep, sure."

"You typed it out exactly like I said it?"

"You were there, dummy. Didn't you see me type it out like you said it? Maybe she doesn't check e-mail that often."

"Yeah, that must be it. Let's write another one."

"Okay, but stop scratching your neck."

"I'm not."

"Yes, you are."

"No, I'm not."

> *Dear Vong,*
>
> *One month ago I am writing you e-mail. I ask you help me to America. You not write back I am waiting you. Maybe now you got baby and you are busy. Or maybe easy job in office and cheese hamburgers make you lazy. Please I am waiting your message.*
>
> *Nok is still okay but she is not laughing my jokes like before.*
>
> *Loving brother,*
> *Seng*

When Nok asked Seng why he wanted to see Vong's New Year card again, Seng just said that he liked the picture on the front. He didn't want to tell her it was so he could make sure they had Vong's e-mail address right. The card showed people skating, which he knew about because he'd seen it on TV. RIDEAU CANAL, OTTAWA was written underneath it. He didn't know where that was, but he was sure he had seen it in an American movie once.

America. Just the name made him feel excited. The land of the free, the home of movie actors with flawless faces; McDonald's, KFC, and all the other fast-food restaurants the communist party didn't allow in Laos; blue jeans; baseball hats and dollars. He wondered how it would be for Nok if he were to leave. Would she miss him? He didn't want to ask her. He was afraid of her blunt response. Besides, he didn't want to say anything until he knew for sure that he was going. He'd send for her as soon as he got there. Vong could pay for her to go to an American university.

Dear Vong,

Another month has gone. You are getting my e-mail? Please let me know you receive or not.
Nok is fine smiling more now. I think I know why. Nana told me falang boy coming to her often.

Loving brother,
Seng

MOTHER WATER

Cam

I ripped open the doors of the massage house. "I can't believe it! Nok? Come check this out."

Some of the other masseuses giggled and were probably glad they didn't have to massage me. By now everyone knew who I was coming to see.

"*Sabaidee*, Cam," Nok said, looking up — perhaps brightly — from the Virginia Woolf book she was reading between customers. Her shiny, black hair flowed long and loose down the back of a pink T-shirt that clung sexily to her lean waist. I wanted to kiss her.

"Get this! I was walking along the street when a dog ran up to me, cocked his leg, and pissed all over my foot. Pissed all over my foot! The bastard picked me out of a crowd and peed on me!"

I was surprised I was cracking up. I was missing a game today because of the fight. Mr. Rose wouldn't even let me practise. Apparently the Thai guard was in hospital with injuries from our brawl.

"It's serious, Cam," Mr. Rose had said.

"He started it."

"You think that matters?"

Seeing Nok seemed to soften it all. I thought maybe she looked glad to see me too. My foot reeked, but for some reason it was hilarious. Obviously I still had a long way to go to quell my temper, but perhaps the laid-back Lao way was rubbing off on me after all. Maybe I was finally beginning to understand this place a bit. Like the importance of peace in the everyday moments. Little things — like someone cutting you off in traffic, or shoving you on the basketball court, or even a dog pissing on your foot — didn't bother people here. They lived by the saying *boh penyang* — "no worries." They saved their energy for telling jokes and helping out friends or family. It seemed kind of simple, yet profound at the same time. Weird how a poor country like Laos can be so rich.

I stopped feeling so peaceful when I saw Nok's face fall. Had she heard about the game?

"That is very bad luck," she said solemnly.

"No kidding! It's kind of funny, though."

"No, Cam. It's a really bad omen." She looked down at the ground.

"What do you mean?" I chuckled nervously.

"It means something bad is going to happen. You must go to the temple. Make some merit and the monk will bless you. After that, the bad luck will be gone."

"Make merit?" I asked.

"So you can be reborn in heaven."

"Kind of like a points system?"

"Maybe. It's for your karma," she said.

"You mean, so I won't come back as a donkey?"

She burst into laughter.

"Karma isn't about punishment; it's about learning all you can in this life so you don't repeat the same mistakes in your next."

"Right, but in my next life I already know not to wear flip-flops that dogs like to piss on."

"Cam!" she tried to look exasperated, but I saw her little amused smile.

I didn't want to belittle Buddhism or her culture, but there was no way I was going to a temple to tell a monk that some dog took a piss on my flip-flops. We didn't say anything, but I did notice that Nok washed my feet twice before massaging them.

As she kneaded my body, I thought about what she'd said. Back home, death was hidden — in the dark, tinted windows of a hearse, in the thick, drawn curtains of a funeral home. Here in Laos, death was in your face: the smoke from a funeral pyre, chickens being readied for supper, a goat hit by a car. It freaked me out a bit, made me think about things.

"Will you show me what to do at the temple?" I asked when the massage was over. Nok hesitated.

"No."

"Why?"

"It's not a good idea for me to be seen around town with you," she said.

"But why?"

"People will think things."

"Is that why you didn't want to come to my game?"

"Yes."

She handed me a cup of sweet jasmine tea. I looked her in the eyes and was struck by how badly I wanted to be with her. All the time. She was something real in my life. Solid. She was truly there, not just pretending to be there. And those full, silky lips. Damn.

Nok looked away from me and started to fold towels hurriedly. Suddenly she stopped.

"Look, if something horrible happens to you, it will be on my conscience. I finish work at five o'clock. Meet me here."

My heart flipped like an acrobat at Vientiane's Russian circus.

❧

Nok was agitated when I met her later that afternoon. She abruptly motioned for me to get on the back of the motorbike she had borrowed from Nana. A girl who rides a motorbike. They're all over the place in Vientiane, but Nok looked extra sexy straddling the black leather seat.

"Are you sure you're okay with this?" I asked, but she already had the engine running.

Her smell, musky and real, joined the breeze whipping at my face as we zoomed down a leafy boulevard. I wanted to wrap my arms around her or lay my hands on top of her thighs so I could feel them tightening and relaxing as she worked the gears. But as we made our way through town, I began to understand her hesitation. Adults leading their cows back home, talking on cellphones, or picking up children after school, all snuck a stare as we scooted by. Some children pointed and called for their friends to have a look. An elderly woman clicked her tongue as she walked across the intersection where we had stopped for a red light. I began to hope the temple wasn't too far.

We pulled up to the front gate of *Wat Sokpaluang*, gaudy and garish with bright yellow-and-red paint peeling off every which way, and fake gold tiles glittering in the harsh sun. I wished I had my sunglasses. I'm sure I looked really cool, squinting like a rat that's just crawled out of its hole.

"Why is everyone looking?" I asked. Even the novice monks couldn't take their eyes off us. "Don't foreigners come to this temple?"

"They think I'm a Thai girl with her client," Nok said frankly, standing taller. She turned and walked into the temple like a dignitary about to make a speech.

"Nok," I touched her shoulder as I followed her. "You don't have to do this."

"I'm not going to taint my merit by refusing to take you to remove the bad omen."

"You're willing to do this, for me?"

She looked away. Then she looked me straight in the eyes. "I am," she said firmly.

A woman at the temple smiled kindly as Nok explained what had happened. She took out skinny, pliable candlesticks and wrapped them like a measuring tape around my head and from my elbow to wrist. We brought the yellow candles to a monk who lit them and let their beeswax drip into a bucket of water filled with yellow and orange flower petals. The monk, draped in a saffron-coloured robe, spoke in Pali. It was the ancient language of Buddhism, Nok said. He tied white strings around our wrists. I was surrounded by beauty — the gentle vibe of the temple, the compassionate brown eyes of the monk, the exotic smell of frangipani, and most of all, Nok. The beauty of this place seemed so pure and genuine. Maybe it really was powerful enough to wipe bad omens away.

As we walked back to the Honda Dream, I asked her if she wanted to go for iced coffee. She looked at me and then laughed.

"Why not? Everyone thinks the worst, anyway," she said, throwing up her arms.

We sat at a dilapidated riverside café, its bamboo balcony threatening to disintegrate into the mocha-coloured Mekong below. The great river ambled lazily between Laos and Thailand. On the opposite banks I spotted Nong Khai. The prosperous Thai town stared across the river at Vientiane, thumbing its well-off capitalist nose at the communists. Apparently Nong Khai was where the Thai guard lay in hospital, with supposed head injuries from our fight. I tried to push him out of my mind — he had already screwed my life up enough. There were rumours at school that I would be suspended for five games and prevented from playing the big tournament in Thailand.

Nok and I talked about everything. She told me about her dream of becoming a sociology professor, and about her hero, Aung San Suu Kyi, a woman who was fighting for democracy in nearby Myanmar.

"I like smart, strong women," she said. "Kind of like your mom."

"Julia? Smart and strong?" I scoffed.

"I see her at the massage house," Nok said. "I think she's brave for moving to another continent with her teenager."

I shrugged.

INSECT NIGHT

Nok

Every day at four in the afternoon, Nok would sneak into the tiny bathroom stall at Fa Ngum Massage and brush her long, dark hair until it gleamed. She didn't want Nana to see her, although she knew her friend already suspected things. Cam came for a massage every day when he was done school. Nok couldn't wait for him to get there. At first she told herself there was no way she was ever going to fall for a *falang*. She didn't think they could be trusted. She was afraid after what had happened to her at the massage house. She still had a creepy feeling that she hadn't seen the last of the foreigner who had tried to attack her.

But Cam was so genuinely interested in her life. Unlike a lot of Lao guys, he didn't have any expectations about what a teenage girl should be doing or thinking. No questions about when she was going to get married or how many babies she wanted. He let her be who she was, and his Western naïveté made her believe that she could do anything. She'd never had a boyfriend before.

"You'll go to university someday," he said, not understanding that there was truly no money. Or time. She had to be working if she and Seng wanted to eat.

"There's got to be a student loan you can get or something."

"No, Cam, not here."

"But you can't give up on your dream. You're too smart."

She loved how he believed in her. He never doubted that her future would be bright. She loved how his freckles dusted his nose like cinnamon on a French cake. The way his strong fingers would reach out to lightly brush her arm when they shared a joke, or how his sandy blonde hair fell into his exotic green eyes.

Last night, after work, they'd walked along the river together, stopping to buy warm cobs of corn from farmers' wives crouched along the banks. She'd linked arms with him and steered him down the bank and closer to the river. It was quiet and dark down there; farther from the road and riverside terraces where people chatted and laughed over beer or mango shakes. No one would spot them. She stopped to wipe a kernel of corn from his chin. She wanted to meet his eyes, but at that moment she couldn't bring herself to. For the first time in her life she felt reticent. He raised a hand to smooth her hair away from her face. She swallowed. Her skin tingled and an unusual kind of warmth rushed over her body. She wanted more, but was afraid of what that meant.

"Cam," she said, and for a split second was unsure if she should ask what was on her mind.

"Yeah?"

"Have you ever had sex?"

His eyes widened.

"Sorry," she said. "I know I can be too direct."

"No, no, it's okay." He paused and looked out over the river. Then he said, "Yes."

She wasn't surprised. "With who?" she asked.

"Drunk, at a party. It was kind of stupid, actually. At the time it felt good, but now I see how fake it was. Just a big act. Kind of explains why I felt depressed the next day." He turned and met her eyes. "Have you?"

"No. Things are slower here — at least for girls."

He looked into her eyes before looking towards the river, dark and slippery in the moonlight.

"So beautiful," he said.

"Wait until you see it all fat and swollen during the rainy season. These banks we're standing on will be covered with water."

"No, I mean you."

She looked at her feet. A fisherman rode by on a creaky, rusty bike. Nok could hear him click his tongue as he eyed the two of them. She gently pulled on Cam's arm so he'd start walking again.

"Do you want to go to Keng Heng?" she asked. The sticky rice was overpriced, but the restaurant usually had a good mix of Lao and foreigners. They wouldn't stand out as much.

The restaurant wasn't far from the river, in a pretty, two-storey colonial villa next to Nam Phou Fountain. The building was a leftover from the days when Laos was a French colony. Now it teemed with Lao NGO workers and their foreign colleagues, scruffy-looking backpackers, United Nations staff, English teachers, and wealthy Lao teenagers craving a glimpse of the world outside of their landlocked country. Western dance music pumped from the stereo. Nok had never been inside before. It was way too expensive for her and Seng. No one she knew would be there.

"Tonight is insect night!" their cheery Lao waiter told them in English as he seated them. "Larvae, grasshoppers, crickets. Do you dare try?"

Nok knew it was an attention-grabber to attract tourists. *Falangs* were always fascinated by what Lao people ate: omelettes with ant eggs, whole frogs barbequed on wooden skewers, duck's-blood soup. They couldn't get over how some Vietnamese living in Laos loved their barbequed dog.

"Uh, okay," Cam said, falling for it.

The waiter brought a round plate to their table of assorted fried insects resting on a pillow of sliced cucumber. Nok laughed as Cam bit gingerly into a crunchy, whole grasshopper.

"I was thinking, maybe —" she started.

Cam spat a barely chewed cricket into his napkin, interrupting her. They laughed out loud.

"Yeah?" he said, wiping his mouth.

"Lao New Year is coming up. There's this party my brother's friend is having. Do you want to come?"

"Of course. You sure it will be okay? I mean, with your brother and all?"

"Well, Seng does like anything Western."

She looked around the room. She noticed a few other mixed couples — Lao and Western.

"Where do you live, anyway?" Cam asked.

"Near That Luang."

"I haven't been there yet."

"You have to go! It's Laos's national symbol. Such a beautiful golden *stupa*."

"What's that?"

"It's a giant, sacred mound, all golden with three tiers. It's supposed to have the Buddha's breastbone inside. During the November full moon there's the That Luang festival. I'll take you there."

For a second she worried that she had said too much, insinuating that they would still be together in November. It was just April, after all. But then she saw Cam's massive grin.

"People come from all over the country for the festival," she continued. "In the morning thousands of people pray together. You can barely even see the *stupa* because of all the people. Women wear their best *sins* and bring alms for the monks and nuns — bananas, *kip*, sticky rice. People push their way through the crowd, selling little birds, like finches or plovers, in homemade cages. You can buy them and let them go. It builds your merit."

He reached across the table and touched her hand. Her immediate reaction was to pull it away, but they would be okay here. Judging by the other couples in the restaurant, it wouldn't be that out of the ordinary. Besides, she was beginning to care less about what other people thought. They sat like that for a while, happy and quiet, until the rest of their meal arrived. Nok looked around the restaurant as their waiter laid out baskets of sticky rice, spicy bowls of *laap*, an overflowing plate of mint, dill, and other leaves picked from the forest or tiny streams, and enormous, steaming bowls of noodle soup.

For a second she wondered if she should eat her sticky rice with her hand, rolling it in a ball in her right hand the way Lao people always do. Do they use cutlery in a place like this? She couldn't imagine how you would eat sticky rice any other way. It would just stick all over a spoon. She was surprised by her insecure thoughts. She decided she wasn't going to change how she had always eaten just because a lot of foreigners happened to be around. She smiled when she saw Cam reach into the basket of rice with his hand. But before she could do the same, her smile vanished.

She looked up to see the *falang* who had mistaken her for a prostitute peering down from the restaurant's second-storey balcony. She could never forget those empty, ice-blue eyes. She pretended she didn't see him, but could tell from her peripheral vision that he wasn't taking his eyes off her. She couldn't concentrate on what Cam was saying.

"We have to go," she stood up too abruptly, knocking over her cup of lemon-grass tea.

"Why? We just got here," Cam said gently, grabbing for napkins before the burning tea crept across the table and onto his lap.

. The foreigner grinned with intent as he met Nok's eyes from the balcony overlooking the restaurant's first floor.

"Just come on!" she grabbed Cam's hand. He looked shocked, but she clenched his hand firmly and led him through tightly spaced tables toward the door. Sweaty backpackers with dreadlocks and dusty clothes, or wealthy Lao women in expensive, shiny *sins* looked up with curiosity from their tables.

"Nok, we have to pay."

By this time the foreigner had come down the polished, wooden stairs and stood right behind her. She grabbed on to Cam's arm and pretended not to notice him. He followed them through the noisy restaurant. The pumping dance music paused briefly before the next song began.

"I knew it," he leaned over and whispered, breathy and heavy, in her ear. He reeked of rice whiskey. He glanced at Cam with glazed, bloodshot eyes and leaned in closer to Nok. "I knew you were a whore the minute I saw you."

"Cam!" Nok screamed and pushed him outside into the heavy humidity of the night. The restaurant door swung shut behind her, leaving the drunken foreigner inside. She raced down Settathirath Road and didn't stop until she was gasping for air. Cam caught up to her.

"Who the hell was that?"

"I have to go home now." She was ashamed beyond words.

"Who was that guy? What did he say?" Cam looked bewildered.

"I'll see you tomorrow, okay?" she said, and turned to hail a *tuk-tuk*. As her heart rate began to slow down, she watched Cam's confused face fade into the distance. The shaky auto rickshaw trundled along, taking her home to be alone with her humiliation. She looked down into her lap and watched the pattern of wet spots her tears made on her *sin*.

By the time the *tuk-tuk* wobbled to a stop in front of her house, her tears had turned into anger. Did that ugly Frenchman see her? Really see her? Did he see that she was a person, just like him? Could he know that she graduated at the top of her class? That she was supporting herself and her brother at the age of sixteen? Her dignity was invisible to him because of her poverty, because her English wasn't perfect, because she was a girl, and because of her brown skin. To him, she was just another thing to buy and use. All he knew about was the money in his pocket and the selfishness in his heart.

She bit on her bottom lip as she counted out *kip* to pay the rickshaw driver. The ride had cost all of the money she had made that day. She wondered why her karma had made this experience necessary. What was she meant to learn? She looked up and saw Seng walking down their laneway with a worried look on his face. They never took *tuk-tuks*.

"Nok?"

He held his hands open at his sides, questioning and offering his support to her at the same time.

"I have a headache, I'm going inside," she said, not meeting his eyes.

He shifted. "I'll get started on dinner, *nong sao*."

She could tell by his tone that he understood something beyond a headache was going on.

She went into their one-room home and curled into a fetal position on the sleeping mat. When Seng called her for dinner she pretended she was asleep. Telling him what had happened would only multiply her shame.

ANGER

Cam

I walked home from the insect restaurant and sat on the front porch, a heavy kind of sadness settling onto me. I didn't even want to play ball when Somchai came by.

"You seem like a creature from outer space," he said.

"Maybe I am," I said. "After all, Canada is on the other side of the world." I looked down at my dirty basketball shoes.

I didn't sleep that night. I kept replaying the scene with the drunk guy in my head to see if there was something I missed that would explain things to me. The next morning I skipped school and went to the massage house instead.

My heart beat faster as Nok came to the entrance and held the door open for me.

"Don't tell me another dog has watered you." Her unique choice of English words made her comment even cuter, but her face looked heavy and drawn.

"Nope, just interested in another hour of satisfaction under the hands of Miss Nok."

She seemed to bristle.

"You mean you'd like a massage?" she asked.

The hot season sun was not the reason for my red face. What else did she think I meant?

"Of course, I meant a massage. What else?" I asked, trying to sound understanding instead of irritated.

"Maybe Nana can massage you today," she said.

Okay, now I was irritated.

"What? Why? Have people been bugging you about being seen with me? Was it that drunk guy last night?"

She shook her head and ran to the staff room upstairs.

"What the hell, Nok? What's going on?" I yelled up the stairs after her. I could feel the anger rising. Maybe she'd had a thing with the drunk guy. Why else was she keeping things from me? She was usually so honest. Nana looked up from her work at the front reception desk and eyed me curiously.

Come on, get it together. Breathe.

I followed Nok upstairs and into the staff room, even though it was for employees only.

"Nok?"

She turned to look at me. Tears flowed like rivers down her cheeks.

"What's going on?" I asked, softening.

"That man, last night? He thinks I'm a hooker," she said, unable to meet my eyes. I sat down beside her and put my arms around her. In between sobs, she told me the story about the attack.

I felt the blood drain from my face. Someone did that? To her?

"What if he comes back, Cam?"

"I will be there," I said. The man would be dead.

"No, Cam. We can't be seen together anymore."

"What?" I felt like she was speaking a different language.

"We just can't. It's not safe."

"Nok, that doesn't make sense."

"He thinks I'm a prostitute and you're my client."

"Who cares what he thinks? We aren't the only mixed couple around Vientiane."

She stood up and wiped her eyes. She crossed her arms and turned her back to me to look out the window.

"You're really upset and scared right now," I said, trying to keep my voice level. "Take some time before you make sudden decisions."

She exhaled loudly. "Look," she said, whipping her head around abruptly so a silken strand of hair caught in her moist lips. "There are some things *falangs* can't understand." She turned her back to me.

So that was it then. I was nothing more than a *falang* to her.

A foreigner. Just like him.

My deep breaths abandoned me. I felt desperate. I was going to lose her. I reached out and grabbed her harshly by the shoulders. Her head jerked until she stood looking at me, shock in her molasses eyes. I wanted to make her understand. Make her see me. See that I was not like him.

"Cam, go. Just go!" she screamed.

I heard Nana coming up the stairs behind me. By then I knew that if there was one thing Lao people didn't like, it was public displays of temper. What the hell was I doing? I loosened my grip.

"I'll never understand you people," I growled as I stomped down the stairs and slammed the flimsy massage-house door shut.

DEATH SLIDE

Cam

I rode my bike home from the massage house as fast as I could and chucked it viciously into the rose apple trees.

"Brother?" Somchai stood at our front gate, his face filled with concern. I ignored him and stomped into the house. I was glad when I heard him follow me.

"What is it?" he asked.

I turned to look at him and was surprised how the worry in his eyes softened everything.

"Nok."

"I told you to be careful with Lao girls. You had a fight?"

"I don't understand anything in this fucking country."

I saw then that I had hurt him. "Sorry, no offence. I just —"

He was quiet for a while. Then he brightened and said, "I know. You need Vang Vieng."

"I don't even know what that is."

"It's a tourist town north of here. Let's go for the weekend. You and me. You'll like it — lots of English there." Somchai grinned.

"But Nok told me Lao New Year is coming up. Isn't it the most important holiday in Laos? You should stay here with Meh Mee," I said.

"We'll just go for a couple days. It'll cheer you up and you'll be ready to party for New Year when we get back."

Getting out of Vientiane sounded good to me. I needed something I could understand. Besides, I didn't feel like being home alone all weekend again. Julia was with the principal all the time now.

The next day after school we took a *tuk-tuk* to the crowded bus station across the road from the Morning Market. Blue buses with JAPAN OFFICIAL DEVELOPMENT ASSISTANCE slapped on the side filled up with people jostling for a seat. Those who couldn't find one just stood. Barefoot kids wearing dirty, buttoned-up shirts and fraying shorts clambered onto the buses carrying plastic bags stuffed with baguettes. "Bread! Fresh bread for sale!" they hollered. Bottles of water were passed through bus windows to passengers already surrendering to the dry season heat. Hmong women with wrinkled faces deep brown with the April sun approached passengers, trying to convince them to buy their colourful cloths. The smell of fried food floated by as elderly women with mouths red from chewing betel nut flogged snacks for the journey. Dust tickled the tip of my nose and settled onto passengers' vintage suitcases that were ripping at the seams. It would be my first time outside of Vientiane. Anticipation should have crowded out thoughts of Nok. But instead I felt so tired. Tired of there being so much that I didn't know and couldn't understand in this country. Tired of my angry past dragging me down like the heavy, breezeless heat. Tired of myself.

The road north to Vang Vieng twisted and curved through the jungle like a roller coaster. We could only find one empty seat on the overcrowded bus and Somchai insisted that I take it. I refused, but he wouldn't sit.

"Take it before we lose it," he said. He hovered over me, his brown hand grabbing on to the bar above as the cheap bus rattled over potholes. He didn't seem to mind the suffocating heat or the other standing passengers elbowing him. He just smiled happily and looked out the window at mango trees and hibiscus bushes whizzing by.

The conductor passed out plastic bags to passengers with their hands held high, like kindergarteners who waited too long to ask to go to the bathroom. I wondered what the bags were for until the little girl in front of me vomited as her older brother held her long hair away from her face. After the next curve in the road, the sound of more puking came from the back of the bus. Disgusted, I looked up at Somchai.

"It's a Lao thing." He shrugged. "Weak stomachs, I guess."

Soon the stench became overpowering. I began to wonder if the trip was a good idea.

I tried not to think about Nok during the ride, but it was impossible. The thought of that French guy forcing himself on her made me so angry I could feel every muscle in my body tighten, like a dog with its hair standing on end. I hoped I would never see him again. I knew it wouldn't be safe for either of us.

My thoughts were interrupted by the bus starting to sputter.

"What's going on?" I asked Somchai. I couldn't stand to be stuck on this barf-mobile for much longer.

"Bus trouble, I guess. *Boh penyang.*"

The bus staggered to a stop. No one seemed concerned but me and the German tourists at the back of the bus.

"I have to get off of this thing."

Somchai followed me down the rickety bus steps to wait outside in the blistering sun. No vehicles zoomed past us on the winding road. We seemed to be surrounded by nothing but jungle. The smell of earth and plants was everywhere, reminding me of the way our kitchen back home smelled when Julia repotted one of her houseplants. For a second I thought of my life back in Ottawa and of Jon and Marissa. I realized that we hadn't been in contact for weeks.

The longer we stood on the jungle's edge, the more I noticed the busyness that lay beneath the peaceful surface of the wilderness around us — birds and insects called out noisily and large animal footprints decorated the road's dusty shoulder. Laos used to be called Lan Xang, the land of a million elephants, although I had yet to see one.

In the distance, I could hear faint singing. It was almost haunting, kind of like the way First Nations people sing back home at pow-wows and stuff.

"It's a tribe," Somchai explained. "An ethnic minority. They sing to let the spirits know they're looking for food."

My body relaxed a bit. I could see the bus driver walking up a dirt path to a small village that sat on top of a lush, green hill. He stopped at the wooden gate of each tiny, thatched roof house and called something out.

"He's seeing if anyone has the tools he needs to fix the bus."

Curious, wild-haired children, some naked, some half-dressed in black clothes with colourful embroidery and silver baubles, emerged tentatively from their homes. A tall, older boy pointed at me. The other kids followed him as he strode toward me. I glanced sideways at Somchai and was glad he was there beside me. He laughed.

"Foreigners always make them curious."

Soon a circle of kids, their mothers watching cautiously from the outskirts, surrounded me.

"*Sabaidee,*" I said, feeling self-conscious. The children roared and their mothers chuckled quietly to the babies tied to their backs.

"They don't speak Lao," Somchai said. "They have their own language."

I nodded as I noticed a man standing behind the women; he wobbled from side to side and appeared to be laughing at nothing. He suddenly pointed at me and started shouting loudly.

"Village drunk, I guess," Somchai said.

"What's he saying?" I asked. The man looked like he was getting more agitated. I thought of Nok's drunk harasser.

"I have no idea."

The man began to stumble toward me. Now he was screaming and wagging a finger at me with hostility. Spit flew from his mouth. I could see his yellowed teeth. One of the mothers was in his way and he shoved her aside force-fully. She fell to the ground and her baby started wailing.

"Hey!" I yelled and advanced toward him. It's what I should have done when the drunk Frenchman was follow-ing Nok. Instead I had just stood there like an idiot, even though I had seen the terror building in her eyes.

"*Boh penyang*, Cam," Somchai was saying. "No worries. He's just a drunk. Let it go." He walked over to the woman and helped her up.

I knew my adrenaline was rising; my tongue felt thicker, the taste in my mouth changed. I looked at the woman dusting off her skirt and straightening up the baby on her back.

"Cam, back off. It's nothing," Somchai urged. He knew all about my fight with the Thai basketball guard. I could see that he was afraid I would hurt someone again.

I tried to slow my breath, making it long and deep. I realized it was my memory from yesterday that was making me so angry, not the present moment. The woman was back to chuckling with her friends. She had obviously let it go. Why couldn't I? A toothless woman tried to distract me by holding up a sort of bamboo flute in front of my face. I let my eyes fall away from the drunk. The woman motioned incessantly for me to play.

Somchai sighed with relief when I took the flute.

What was I, the Pied Piper? I'd never played an instrument before, unless you count the piano lesson Julia forced me to go to when I was ten. Her attempt to refine me. I had gone to the first lesson to try to keep her happy, but it didn't last long. Halfway through, the teacher mumbled something about me being tone deaf. I stormed out and never went back.

Now there was no running away. It seemed the entire village and bus were watching me. I had no choice but to take the flute. No one else seemed to be as bothered by the drunk as I was. I blew into the instrument hesitantly and it made a sound like a smoker's cough. The crowd started to chuckle tentatively. The man waved his hand at me as if he was dismissing something and mumbled to himself as he wandered off. I watched him turn around and pee into the bushes. The children laughed.

By now other bus passengers had their faces pressed to the windows, or had come off the bus to see what was happening. I put the flute up to my mouth to play again, when, like an unexplainable character that pops out of nowhere in the midst of a bizarre dream, a wizened old woman appeared, wearing a pair of Ray Ban sunglasses that were too big for her face with rhinestones stuck to the black arms. Her sunglasses seemed so out of place in this practically prehistoric village. It was so wacky I couldn't resist. I laughed out loud. She ignored my laughter, took the flute from me, clicked her tongue, and began to play an energetic tune that sounded like the jungle insects. The children laughed and clapped and danced. I felt like I was in the middle of a photo from *National Geographic*. My fear about losing Nok eased up a little. I would find a way to make it okay again. In a culture as fluid and open-hearted as this, anything was possible.

I was almost disappointed when the bus driver finished his work underneath the belly of the old bus, and motioned for everyone to get back on. I could have hung out here for a while. The drunk was nowhere in sight. As I settled back into my hard seat, I heard a German girl call out from the back of the bus.

"Hey, has anyone seen my sunglasses?"

"Black with rhinestones?" Somchai answered.

"Yeah, that's them."

As the bus pulled away, he pointed out the window to the wrinkled, old flute player, wearing the sunglasses and now doing some kind of funky jig with the children as she played. Even the German girl couldn't help but laugh.

The bus started its roller-coaster ride again. The driver passed back more plastic barf bags. By the time we got to Vang Vieng I was too woozy to worry that we were nowhere but on the side of some country road, surrounded by craggy mountains closing in on me like the bodies on the bus. In a daze, I followed Somchai along the path into Vang Vieng town.

It wasn't long before I was yanked out of my foggy brain. I couldn't believe the number of foreigners in one spot. Bands of white guys with sunburned shoulders joked with each other in English as they walked by. Tanned European girls in tiny bikinis rode their rented bicycles through the handful of streets while Lao men giggled and Lao women shifted in discomfort. A group of Israelis kicked a *katoh* ball as their Hebrew floated through the countless restaurants. I overheard a fat *falang* attempting to explain to a waitress the meaning of "over easy."

Somchai chuckled as he watched my jaw drop.

"You like?" he asked.

I didn't know yet. It was such a shock after our stop in the jungle village. I felt like someone had chucked a bucket of cold water on me.

We found a guesthouse and unpacked before going back outside. We passed a shop renting inner tubes and he asked if I wanted to get one and float down the River Song, which flowed along the edge of the small tourist town. I shrugged. I didn't know why, but I wasn't sure about this place, even though I could understand nearly every conversation that wafted past me. The familiarity of Western culture everywhere should have made me feel better, but it didn't.

I followed Somchai into the inner tube shop, anyway, and then down to the riverbank. Water buffalo watched us from muddy banks as we drifted downstream in the cheap, black tubes. I could see why tourists were into this. Warm river water flowed between my toes. Vibrant blue-and-yellow butterflies gathered together in the riverbank reeds. Jagged mountains loomed overhead like lifeguards in a chair. We hadn't gone far when an old man called to us from one of the banks. He held out a large stick for us to grab on to. I looked at Somchai, confused.

"It's his business," he explained. "He brings the tourists in so they can see the caves on this side of the river. Grab on."

I caught the elderly man's stick and he pulled me in towards the bank. We paid him 1000 *kip* and he gave us a flashlight so we could see inside the cave. Climbing the trail to the cave, massive leaves waved us on and red ants scurried for a taste of our hands as we placed them on a rickety bamboo handrail. I was back in my lush, jungle dream. The only thing missing was Nok.

The mouth of the cave was cool and dark and it took a minute for my eyes to adjust. I turned on the flashlight and followed the path inside. Somchai was right behind me. Water echoed loudly as it dripped from the cave's ceiling, making the rocks slick and wet. The air smelled dank and stagnant. We crept along barefoot, our fingers running along the cave's slippery walls so we wouldn't lose our bearing. I could barely see a thing.

Somchai whispered something about a Buddha statue being deep inside. His voice reverberated in the hollowness and garbled what he said. I turned around to ask him to say it again when I lost my footing. I fell with a thud against a sharp rock and heard something crack. Then I began to slide. Farther and farther into the cave, pointy rocks stabbing and piercing me all the way down. Lightning rods of pain shot through my body, but everything was moving so quickly I couldn't tell which parts were being damaged. I saw splotches of red on my running shoes as I began to somersault. First I saw the cave's slick ceiling, then the floor. Ceiling, floor, ceiling, floor. I tumbled farther down the death slide. A metallic taste rose in my mouth and by body was stiff with fear. I heard Somchai's voice call my name, but it was getting fainter. I was completely disoriented, when my head slammed into a rock and everything went black.

GRATEFUL HEAD

Seng

Seng was going to meet Khamdeng at their usual spot along the riverbank. He asked Nok if she wanted to come along. He loved being seen with her. She was known around their village for her smarts and determination. All of the girls envied her tall, proud way. They knew that someday she would make Laos proud. But Nok didn't want to come with him. He wondered if she was embarrassed. Maybe walking beside him made her feel dragged down. He was a big weight on his sister's success.

"What's wrong, little sister?"

She shook her head. "Nothing."

"You, hiding things? That's not normal."

He decided it was time to mention what Khamdeng had told him.

"You've been hanging around a *falang* boy?"

She looked up abruptly. "How did you know?"

"Khamdeng saw you. By the river."

She nodded. Seng's heart flipped. Nok with a boyfriend! And a foreign one at that. They were America-bound for sure!

"Which state is he from? California? New York? Connecticut? Montana? Iowa? Washington? Delaware? Minnesota —"

"Are you going to name all fifty states again?"

"North Carolina? South Carolina? Arkansas? Massachusetts?"

"Seng!"

"Sorry. But I know them all, you know."

"I know."

"So, which?"

"He's not American," she said.

"So sorry to hear that."

"He's Canadian."

Seng didn't know a thing about Canada.

"It's next to America," Nok explained. "Not as many people, lots of forests and snow, French and English."

Close enough, Seng thought. "Do they eat cheese?"

She laughed and gave him a playful shove. At least he could still make her smile.

"Now I know why you won't hang out by the river. You're going to see Canada Boy."

She looked down at the ground and shrugged. "You go, Seng. I'll see you when you get back."

He walked toward the Mekong with a bounce in his step. Why hadn't he thought of this before? A foreign boyfriend for his little sister. It was perfect. Now she would be less serious and have a shot at something better than the massage house, although she would argue that she didn't need a guy for success. She didn't need Seng, that was for sure. He began to wonder if she would leave him like Vong had, but then he spotted Khamdeng sitting under a coconut tree and throwing pebbles into the Mekong. It made him think of loyalty. Of course Nok wouldn't leave him. She was different.

"What's up with your shirt?" Khamdeng asked, pointing to his new, pink T-shirt.

"You like it? Grateful Head. It's a super cool American band."

"It's the Grateful Dead, you dimwit."

"No, it isn't."

"Yes, it is."

"No, it isn't."

"Yes it is. And they're an old band. Not cool anymore."

"Then why would they make a Grateful Head T-shirt?" Seng asked. "I got it at the Morning Market."

"The Morning Market isn't exactly on the pulse of what's cool. They put all kinds of messed-up English on shirts."

Seng wasn't going to let Khamdeng's disapproval ruin this great day. Nok had a boyfriend! A *falang* boyfriend! Seng wondered if the guy had a sister. Maybe they could double date.

A group of tourists rode by on rented bicycles. Seng suddenly wished he had brought some plastic goods to sell.

"Hey, the Grateful Head!" one of the guys stopped and pointed at Seng. His friends stopped, too, and they laughed when they saw Seng's T-shirt.

"Told you," Khamdeng said.

"That's awesome!" a tourist laughed.

"See?" Seng said to Khamdeng. "I am on the pulse." *I'll wear this next time I work*, he thought.

The backpackers asked where they could go for good food. They stood chatting with Seng and Khamdeng for awhile; wondered where they could get a T-shirt like

Seng's. He gave them directions to the Morning Market. Then one of them leaned in closer, lowered his voice.

"Speaking of head," he said, a grin on his face. "I've heard about Southeast Asia. Know where I can get some?"

"What do you mean?" Seng looked at him blankly. Khamdeng shifted.

"You know. Head. I heard you can get it cheap in a poor place like this. At those massage houses."

Khamdeng stepped forward. "A massage house isn't a brothel," he said and Seng could hear the resentment in his friend's voice. Suddenly the ugliness of the tourists' words dawned on him.

"You're an ass, Will," one of the tourist's friends said to him. "It's cheap because the place is poor. Those girls don't have another option. You want to take advantage of that?"

Will raised one shoulder. "I was just asking. You know you hear all those stories. I'm just curious, that's all."

"Let's go eat," the other backpacker said in an annoyed tone.

Seng watched as they rode away, his heart suddenly feeling heavy in his chest. If he wasn't so fat, he'd rip his stupid T-shirt off.

BOH PENYANG

Cam

My head seared with pain as I came to consciousness.
My eyes felt like lead as I slowly opened them. I don't
know why I even bothered — blackness was everywhere.
I couldn't see a thing. I felt hard, wet protrusions digging
into my spine. The air around me smelled dank and rot-
ten. My body tensed with fear as I frantically searched my
throbbing brain to try to remember where I was.

"Nok?" I tried to call out in a hoarse voice. But even as
I said it I knew it wasn't the right name. She wouldn't be
there. Who would be? I couldn't remember.

I began to panic. My legs felt restless and jumpy, but
I couldn't move them. I felt sweat trickling down my
forehead, but I shivered with dampness and cold at the
same time. My breath was shallow and quick, like a dog
panting. I could taste blood in my mouth.

"Hello?" I called out. My voice echoed eerily. When it
stopped I heard nothing except for the continuous dripping of water. The sound made me remember.

I was in the cave.

"Somchai?"

Silence.

The whir of wings flapping fluttered past my left ear. Bats.

I was desperate for something to drink. I wondered how close the dripping water was. Could I open my mouth and let some drops fall in? I tried to shift my body, but a blaze of pain stopped me. I could do nothing but lie in the stillness and feel my heart rage against my ribcage.

It seemed like hours passed. Where did Somchai go? I was alone in the dark with no clue about when he would come back, and no power to help myself. It made me remember Julia's date nights when I was a kid. I tried to deepen my breath, but it hurt my ribs too much when my lungs expanded. I wished I could close my eyes and sleep.

I would have given anything to be back home; not in Ottawa, but back in our rented house in Vientiane. I wanted to find Nok and tell her how sorry I was for grabbing her like that. I wanted to walk with her by the river and forget all about the drunk guy, the basketball fight, and my mother.

My bladder felt like it was going to explode. I had to pee so badly, but I couldn't move. I tried to shift to my right side so the piss would run down the cave path, mixing with its slickness, but I couldn't do it. Suddenly, I felt a rush of warm liquid and wetness between my legs. I felt anger rising up my body, but I had no way to release it. I couldn't move. It rose and rose until I felt like a balloon about to pop. I screamed long and loud. Why would Somchai leave me alone?

I was about to go berserk when I thought I saw light flashing along the ceiling of the cave. A bat whizzed past me. The light started to bob up and down. Then I heard someone calling out in Lao, but I couldn't understand what they were saying.

"I'm here!" I yelled. "Over here!"

More indecipherable Lao reverberated off the cave walls. I heard footsteps quickening their pace. I could tell someone was almost upon me. I was flat on my back, my head pointed in the direction of the footsteps, but I couldn't turn to see who was behind me. I was so powerless. It didn't sound like Somchai's voice.

Suddenly a headlight seared my eyeballs. When it moved off to the side it took my eyes a while to adjust to the darkness that was left behind. I saw a stranger wearing a massive, old-fashioned pair of glasses that looked almost clownish on his small, brown face. I attempted to sit up, but he pushed me back down.

"He's a doctor," I heard Somchai say from behind, and then felt a reassuring hand on my shoulder. A rush of relief flooded my body. My breath returned. He came back.

We sat in the darkness, Somchai holding a Thermos of cool water to my lips every so often, as he and the doctor debated what to do. I had never tasted water so refreshing and sweet. Suddenly there were more shouts and footsteps.

"Some villagers offered to follow us in case we needed more help," Somchai explained. "They're coming now."

I could hear an animated conversation happening behind me, but I couldn't understand any of it. It sounded like two more men were there.

"They're going to make a stretcher so we can carry you out," Somchai said.

"Make a stretcher?" I said in a weak, whispery voice.

"Yeah, there's a clinic in Vang Vieng, but they're not well equipped."

More hours seemed to pass. My body convulsed with cold. Somchai had wrapped a blanket around me, but it didn't seem to be helping. He patted my shoulder.

"It won't be much longer, brother," he said. He looked worried.

Finally the men arrived. Somchai lifted me up by the shoulders and the doctor placed his arms underneath me to support my back. Pain shot through my entire body. They laid me on the makeshift stretcher. From what I could tell it was made from some long poles of bamboo and material like a woman's *sin*. My brain pounded against my skull.

When we came out of the cave the sunlight was unbearably intense. The men loaded me on to a long-tail boat and we rowed across the river. Flies buzzed around me as my skin began to slowly cook in the sun. I could hear the rhythmic dipping of the oars into the river.

"We're going to the clinic, Cam. They don't have much, but they will see what they can do," Somchai said.

The clinic was nothing but one bare room with some hospital-green cabinets in a corner, and one light bulb dangling from the ceiling. They laid me on the floor in the stretcher. The doctor took out his penlight and began to examine my broken body.

"Concussion. Sprained ankle. Three cracked ribs," Somchai called out my injuries as the doctor explained them to him. Just the sound of his voice was assurance that everything was going to be okay. "You will be in pain for a while, but you're going to be okay, brother. The doctor says you will heal."

I took a deep breath of relief.

"There's just one thing," Somchai said, wincing slightly.

"What?" I asked, afraid of the look on his face.

"You need stitches in your chin."

"Okay, that's not so bad, considering."

"Well," Somchai began. "The good news is that they do have suture thread here at the clinic."

"And the bad news?"

"They don't have anesthetic."

I swallowed.

"Can the stitches wait?" I asked.

"For what?"

"Until we get back to Vientiane?"

"Brother, I am sorry, but you aren't going to be ready to travel back to Vientiane for a few days. We are going to miss most of Lao New Year." He looked away. I knew that to him it was the equivalent of missing Christmas.

"Oh, man," I said. "Your sister is coming, right? From Thailand."

"I'm not leaving you here, Cam."

"Thank you," I said, and I meant it.

The doctor prepared the stitches. I pressed my lips together. As he approached me I could see the flash of the silver needle. I flinched. The doctor said something to Somchai.

"Brother, it is important that you stay as still as possible. Here, I will hold your hand."

I felt like a child as he rubbed the top of my hand and then took it in his. He began to sing softly. I felt the sharp sting of a needle puncturing my flesh.

"It's my favourite Lao folk song," Somchai began to talk quickly, trying to distract me. "It's about farmers who have nothing. Their fields won't grow."

The needle pierced me, stinging each time it moved in and out, in and out. I clenched my toes. The pain seared from my chin all the way down to my groin. It was all I could do not to scream.

"But the farmers are not sad. Instead they dance in a *lam vong* circle with their families. Everything is okay," Somchai continued.

I thought of Jon and the basketball guys back home. I couldn't remember experiencing friendship quite like this. My heart swelled with a kind of love that I had never felt for a friend before. Finally the doctor pulled away from me.

"It's finished," Somchai said. Then he negotiated with the doctor to buy some crutches. I saw some money pass between them. Then I remembered. This wasn't Canada; there was no public health care here. All of this was costing Somchai. He must have had to pay all that he could to get the doctor to come to the cave. I would pay him back, but for right now the bills in my pocket were soaked with my own piss.

I wrapped one arm around Somchai and leaned on the crutch on my left side. Together we hobbled to our guesthouse, moving as slowly as a farmer after a long day in a sweltering rice paddy. That night I slept fitfully. Every time I woke Somchai was there, sitting at the foot of my bed reading Thai comics.

"Need some water?" he asked. I propped myself up as he held a straw to my mouth.

"Go to sleep," I murmured.

"The doctor said I have to watch you because you've had a concussion."

"Come on, Somchai. You've done enough. Sleep — otherwise you'll look like an old man and you'll never be able to find a girlfriend."

"Don't be so sure of that," he said, and gave my arm a playful shove.

My body felt a lot better by the next night, but lying in bed doing nothing was making me replay the scene with Nok and the drunk guy over again. Would she still want me to go to the Lao New Year party with her? I remembered the night she'd clutched my hand underneath the table of the riverside café. If only we could hit rewind and start again from there.

I needed some air. Somchai held on to me as I tried to get used to the crutches.

"Let's go for a walk," I said.

Somchai laughed. "Not yet, brother. Take it easy."

The next day I tried the crutches again.

"Come on, let's go," I said. "I'm going mental just lying here."

Somchai laughed. "Sitting still gives you *falangs* a nervous tic, doesn't it?"

"I can't stop thinking about her." I was beginning to hate the word *falang*.

"Okay, come on then," Somchai said, giving in.

We hobbled out to the main road. I could barely open my eyes in the bright sun. My body was stiff and ached everywhere, but it felt good to be outside. We walked some more and I paused to catch my breath. Three sweaty, shirtless guys walked past with Canadian flags sewn onto their backpacks. The flags caught my eye. I made eye contact with one of them.

"Where are you from?" I asked, leaning forward on the crutches and pointing my chin towards the flag.

"Edmonton. You?"

"Ottawa."

"Been in Vang Vieng long?"

"A couple days. This is my friend, Somchai. We live in Vientiane."

"You live there? That's cool, man. I'm Jake. We're going to get something to eat. Want to come?"

Somchai looked at me with a grin. I knew he'd think it would be a great chance to practise his English.

"Do you want to eat here or there?" Jake pointed at two nearby restaurants. *Nudee Restaurant* sat right beside *Give Pizza a Chance.* I noticed a sign out front with the painted words: NEED TO GET DRUNK? GET DRUNK LAO STYLE! Something about it made me feel depressed, although the beer went down really nicely. The inside of the restaurant was dim and shadowy compared to the garish sun outside. Before I knew it a parade of empty bottles stood in front of me and I was bragging about my fight with the Thai basketball guard. Somchai sat silent beside me, obviously not understanding the slang and the quick pace of the conversation. I didn't bother slowing things down or explaining to him. I don't know if it was the beer, or because I was so hungry for easy, English conversation with someone who understood my culture. Whatever it was, I needed this. Besides, now he knew how I felt in Vientiane.

"You smoke? I've got some good stuff I bought from an old lady on the way here," Jake said.

Normally I wasn't into weed. It turned the next day's basketball game into crap. But I was still suspended and couldn't play ball for weeks. And I really wanted to get away from everything — just for tonight. Besides, the throbbing in my ankle and ribs was making me crazy.

"Yeah. Pass it over," I slurred.

Somchai looked at me blankly. Then he leaned over and whispered, "Do you think that's a good idea, brother? I mean after the concussion and all."

I shrugged and took a swig of beer.

"Is that your mother?" one of the guys asked, gesturing toward Somchai.

I didn't say anything. The other guys laughed. Somchai sat there for a while, his massive smile fading like the setting sun, and watched us pass the joint around the thick, wooden table.

"I take it you don't want any?" Jake said when it came time to pass it to Somchai.

Somchai turned to me. "Cam, I'm tired. I'm going back to the guesthouse."

"Suit yourself."

"What'd he say?" the drunkest guy asked. "I can barely understand him."

I don't know if it was the alcohol, drugs, or hunger for a taste of back home that made me laugh with the others. Even as the sound left my lips a self-hatred flared inside that the pot couldn't douse.

I sat, numbly unaware of the conversation eddying around me in the dark, beer-smelling room. Finally I couldn't bear myself anymore. I got up to leave, but I stumbled forward as I grabbed for my crutches. I knocked some bottles off the table.

"Whoa, a little bit drunk, eh, Vientiane guy?" Jake said, laughing.

"It's my ankle. I sprained it," I said, trying to stand upright.

No one passed me my crutches. No one asked if they could help. They just all sat there, watching me with drunk, stupid looks on their faces. I staggered back to the guesthouse on my own, but Somchai wasn't there.

The next morning the sunlight temporarily blinded me as it gushed through the worn drapes of our cheap guesthouse room. Somchai didn't look me in the eye when he came into the dingy room carrying clear plastic bags filled with *nam wan*.

"Good for hangover," he said.

"Somchai, I —"

"It's okay, Cam," he said, pronouncing my name like the Lao word for gold. "I know it's the *falang* way."

I closed my eyes. I didn't know what hurt more, my head or my heart.

Dizzy and dry-mouthed, I eventually followed him outside to find a place to eat breakfast, even though it was well past lunch. We passed a group of tourists trying to negotiate a cheaper rental price for an inner tube. They kind of looked ridiculous. To them, the cost would have been the equivalent of one beer. Meanwhile the store-owner probably could have bought a day's worth of food for his family for the same amount. The guys had no shirts and one of the girl's bra straps fell out of her tight tank top. Another had underwear peeking out from her short-shorts. Normally I liked getting a glimpse of bra straps and panties. But the tourists looked oversized and tacky next to the classy Lao women in their tailored *sins* and Lao families working their butts off in the oppressive sun.

"Forget breakfast. Let's walk," I said to Somchai. My ankle was killing me, but I was afraid that if I stopped

I would somehow melt into this place. I'd assimilate so there would be no difference between them and me.

"You don't even ask me if I want to walk. You just assume I'll follow you," he said.

I stood there, shocked. I didn't know what to say. I'd never seen Somchai angry before.

Then he turned and began walking anyway. I toddled behind him. We walked for a long time. I tried to think of a way to make things better, to make him see that I wasn't like that, but I didn't know how to without sounding like an idiot. The guy would do anything for me, absolutely anything, and I had treated him like crap.

As we walked in silence out of the tourist area and into the surrounding village, it looked like there was a lot of commotion happening for a sleepy Lao neighbourhood. Groups of women sat on their haunches in the shaded spaces that existed underneath houses built on stilts for air flow and flood protection. They hacked at papayas and chopped tomatoes, cilantro, and carrots. Women walked by wearing shiny *sins* with gold or silver thread and men wore crisp, starched cotton shirts with Nehru collars. A Buddha image covered with garlands of orange flowers sat outside a dilapidated temple with lazy smoke winding its way up from a stick of incense burning at its feet. The thick scent of the incense mixed with the smell of spring rolls frying. I noticed there weren't any tourists, even though the village was only minutes from the guesthouses.

My mind was busy beating myself up for how I had treated Somchai when suddenly a gang of barefoot boys attacked me with Super Soaker water guns.

"Sabaidee Pi Mai!" they screamed, laughing wildly and shooting me without remorse.

Somchai smiled for the first time since the night before. He saw the stunned look on my face. The hard stream of water torpedoing out of the boys' guns pounded my cheek relentlessly. I winced.

"Lao New Year," he explained. "They're washing off the old to be clean for the new." Then he looked off in the distance and mumbled, "I should be home with my family."

Balanced on my crutches, I wiped my soaking-wet face with my forearm. "Instead you're here with me."

Somchai didn't say anything. A stream of ice-cold water pummelled my back. Finally, the boys fled to find their next victims, leaving me drenched and standing in a puddle of mud that had formed at my feet. I could still hear them calling out to each other in excited, breathless voices, making plans for their next attack, as they rounded the corner, leaving Somchai and me alone. I turned to him.

"Look, I was a real ass last night," I said. "It's not the *falang* way."

He shrugged and left me to hobble back to the guest-house alone.

ALONE

Seng

Seng was so excited for the Lao New Year party at Khamdeng's house. He was wearing his best shirt, the one that Nok had saved up a month's salary to buy. The last button was missing, but he didn't think anyone would notice. He hadn't worn his Grateful Head T-shirt again. It suddenly seemed very ugly.

Nok was wearing one of the *sins* Vong had left behind. She looked pretty in the purple matching top, even though the tailor had sewn it for Vong, who was pudgier.

"Didn't you say your *falang* boy was coming with us?" he asked as they walked up Khamdeng's laneway. Now he was even more eager for Nok's foreign romance to happen. He realized how badly she had to get out of the massage house.

"Cam isn't coming," she said.

"So sorry to hear that." Seng tried not to look too disappointed. He wanted to quiz the guy about visas to America. Surely a Canadian would know about that kind of stuff. "Why not?"

She shrugged. "I was stupid."

"Why?"

"It's complicated, you know. Lao and *falang*."

He didn't know, but he wanted to find out. Going out with a foreign girl would be his dream come true.

"It's only as complicated as you make it," he said.

"I know. You're right."

I am right? he thought. *I can give her advice?* He stood a little taller.

"I think I made a big mistake," she said.

"I can see your heart is hurting, little sister."

She nodded and he could see her eyes starting to get watery. He pulled her in toward his chest.

"Is it too late to fix it?" he asked, hopeful.

She smiled. "No." She wiped her eyes and raised her chin. "It's not."

Just then Khamdeng's brother came out. "*Sabaidee Pi Mai!* Come in! Come in! Everyone is here."

Together they walked into the massive tent Khamdeng's father had rented for the party. Guests sat in small circles on plastic chairs under the tent to shield them from the hot April sun. The blue, yellow, and red canvas reflected onto their sweaty faces as the temperature rose. They laughed and shared jokes while eating forkfuls of *laap*, fried rice, and Lao salad. People dressed in their best clothes wove through the crowd with buckets of perfumed water, pouring them down each other's backs and wishing each other a happy Lao new year. Seng was giddy with anticipation. *Pi Mai* was his favourite time of year.

"You're looking handsome," Khamdeng's mother said to Seng as she poured water down his back. "*Sabaidee Pi Mai!*"

"Happy New Year to you too!"

A man shouted overtop of the blaring music and encouraged people to start dancing.

Khamdeng circled the party, pouring shots of strong rice whiskey for everyone. If a woman refused, her husband, brother or male friend would have to drink her share. If someone said the alcohol was disgusting he would have to drink an extra shot. If someone said the alcohol was good he would have to drink an extra shot for lying. It was the way drinking was done in Laos. Seng always had to drink Nok's share, but he never minded. She made sure he got home safely at the end of the night.

Khamdeng continued to circle the party with the bottle and the shot glass until the *lao-lao* was nearly gone. Not wanting his friend to lose face by running out of alcohol, Seng offered to take Khamdeng's motorbike to pick up some more.

Nok overheard. "Are you joking again? You're too drunk and you know it. You're not even good at riding a motorbike sober."

Seng called Khamdeng over to pour a shot for Nok.

"*Muht*! All! Drink it all!"

She drank the bitter liquid and he laughed, until he slowly realized that she only drank it because she knew it would be his if she refused. She smiled weakly at Khamdeng and he saw that his friend didn't want to be pouring it any more than she wanted to be drinking it. He suddenly felt like throwing up.

"Seng! You are not getting on that bike."

"*Boh penyang*, little sister. Don't worry. Why are you always so serious? It's *Pi Mai*! Hey, I just had an idea."

"Here we go," she said, rolling her eyes.

"I'm not an idiot," he said, standing up to her for the very first time. He saw the look of surprise on her face.

"Seng, I'm not saying you're an idiot."

"But that's what you were thinking."

"No it isn't."

"Let's pick up Canada Boy on our way," he said. "You can say sorry and make things okay."

He saw her brighten.

"See, I'm not an idiot. Do you know where he lives?"

She nodded. "But let me drive."

"You don't always have to rescue me, Nok." It felt good, saying what he really thought.

"Okay, fine. You're not an idiot, Seng. That's not what I meant. But if something happens to you I will be alone."

"I'm going to look after you always, little sister."

Nok rolled her eyes and said, "*Oi*! You mean I'm going to look after you always." She playfully slapped him on his sweaty back. She climbed onto the back of the Honda Dream.

Seng liked the feel of his sister's strong body balanced on the seat behind him. Her confidence somehow gave him confidence. With her he was somebody. The sound of the motorbike starting drowned out the music of the dancers.

The night air felt good whipping across his face. It cooled him down. It was so hot underneath that tent. He decided to go a little faster. Nok tightened her grip behind him. He could feel the bumps of the road vibrating his body. His love handles jiggled and it made him laugh out loud. If only he could have a motorbike like this. He'd have to sell a lot of plastic combs and buckets to be able to afford it. Someday. In America he'd have a big, loud Harley-Davidson.

He decided to turn onto a quiet side road just in case the traffic police were out tonight. They didn't care much about drunk drivers — everyone in Laos did it now and then — but Seng had noticed the new government banners strung across Lan Xang Boulevard. In bright red characters they bellowed out a new campaign to stop drunk driving. Must be some new policy the government had come up with to appear more modern. He had seen American ads on TV telling people not to drive after partying.

As he completed the turn onto the quiet, gravel road, he noticed a truck up ahead. It looked like it was coming right at them. It looked too big to be on a little road like this one. And why was it on the wrong side? He felt Nok tapping on his back. He turned to the side to try to hear what she was saying, but the wind took away her words.

When he looked back the truck was even closer. Seng could smell its diesel, but its lights were so bright he had to squint. Nok started hitting his back forcefully.

"What?" he yelled, turning slightly to try to see her in his peripheral vision, but as he did he saw her fall off the back of the motorbike. She slid off easily, like someone slipping into a pond for a swim. He couldn't see her face, just her long hair flailing around violently in the wind. Then she was gone.

There was a flash of light and he turned to see the truck upon him. He could see the terror in the driver's eyes. Seng swerved the bike sharply to the side and fell into a ditch. The truck screeched to a halt.

He could hear blood pumping in his brain. Everything seemed to be happening in slow motion. He jumped off his bike and raced toward his sister, expecting to see her dusting off her *sin*. He was an idiot. Such a big, stupid idiot. He saw a brilliant halo of blood circled around her head. Her eyes were open, looking off to the side, frozen in terror. He knelt down and placed his fingers in her warm blood spilling over the dirt road.

"Nok?" he shook her shoulders gently. Her body was limp.

"Nok!" he screamed. He placed his ear to her chest, wanting to hear the rhythm of her heart, or the waves of her breath. There was nothing. Her body was absolutely still. Suddenly the truck's horn began to blare continuously. Seng was hopeful that someone had arrived to help. He looked up and saw the driver slumped up against the wheel.

"No!" He held his hand up to his mouth. "No!" His entire body began to quake. He tasted salt in his mouth and turned into the bushes to heave. He looked around desperately for someone to help him. There was nothing on the silent street except for the passed-out truck driver and some rice paddies. He went back to his little sister and gently closed her eyelids with his shaking finger. He leaned over and kissed her on the forehead, inhaling deeply, trying to commit her smell to memory.

Then he turned and ran as fast as he could into the bush, leaving her broken and alone on the ground, her quiet confidence split open on the street. He ran with all of his might. He would run until he found someone who could bring his sister back.

WAIT

Cam

Each time the bus back to Vientiane careened over a pot-
hole, pain radiated from my ribs throughout my entire
body. I tried to brace myself each time it looked as if we
were going to hit a bump, but the stiffening of my body
only made the hurting worse. The wound on my chin
was puffy and thin; red lines were snaking up from it
toward my jaw. I wondered if it was infected.

Somchai sat on the hard, metal seat across from me
looking out the window. He had only said a few sentences
to me since two nights ago when I'd gotten high. When he
smiled at the bus conductor or the three children crammed
into the seat behind him it seemed forced. I leaned across
the bus aisle toward him.

"Hey," I said. "What are you thinking about?"

"My sister."

"Will she be there when we get back?"

"No, she'll be back in Thailand by now. She has to
work tomorrow."

"She doesn't get a holiday for Lao New Year? There's

still one day of *Pi Mai* left, right?"

"This weekend was her holiday. It was my only chance to see her. She cleans rooms at a Thai hotel. Hotels don't boot all of their guests out for New Year."

"Somchai, I really am sorry," I said, swallowing the lump pressing on my throat.

"I know you are."

"Damn, I have a lot of making up to do. First Nok, now you. What is wrong with me?"

Somchai didn't say anything. He looked out the window. After a while he leaned across the aisle and said, "It's all about you, Cam."

"What do you mean?"

"You put yourself first all the time. It's all about how you feel and what you want."

His words stung. I didn't know what to say. I sat quietly, shocked and hurt.

"Is that supposed to make me feel better?" I finally asked, snappy and irritated.

"No. I'm not trying to make you feel better. You asked me what was wrong with you."

"In English that's usually meant as a rhetorical question."

"Rhetorical?"

"You're not meant to answer it."

"Why bother asking it in the first place, then? I'm just saying, you can never be happy that way."

I shifted in my seat. I didn't like what he was telling me.

"So why are you always so happy then, Mr. Fucking Sunshine?"

"I'm not perfect," he said. "All I know is that I feel good when I think of something bigger than myself."

I met his eyes.

"I mean, it's good to know what you like and want in this world, but focusing on yourself all the time can drive you crazy. That's why all you Western people are depressed," he said.

"We're not all depressed."

He shrugged. "You're all about the individual. Here we put the family or community first."

"And that's working out real well for you, isn't it? You're going to flunk out of school because you have to make money for your family."

"I'm not saying it's faultless, I'm just saying —" He sat and thought for a second, "maybe there's a middle way between serving you all the time and serving others."

I sat quietly, unable to think of a defence.

He turned to tickle the kid in the seat behind him who had been pulling on his little neck hairs throughout our entire conversation.

I looked out the bus window.

"Are you going to go see Nok when we get back?" he asked, breaking the thick silence between us as we got closer to Vientiane.

"I don't know if this is a good time. I feel like crap."

"Don't let any more time pass. There are lots of handsome guys in Vientiane. Like me."

I held in a laugh only because it would make my ribs hurt.

As the bus barrelled along jungle roads, scarcely missing emaciated village dogs crossing the street, and bands of children wheeling frayed bicycle tires along the roadside with sticks, I played over in my head how I would apologize to Nok. By the time the bus belched us out in

Vientiane, I was groggy from the concussion, the winding roads, and thinking about what Somchai had said. Maybe I did think about myself too much. I wouldn't go to the massage house right away. I'd go home, sleep off Vang Vieng, and go to apologize in the morning.

"Go now," Somchai urged, slapping me on the back. "Maybe she'll think crutches are sexy."

"Why do you put up with me?" I asked.

"Because that's what friends do," he said.

"You Lao take your friendships seriously."

"Most important thing," he said. Then he turned his back and walked toward a colony of *tuk-tuk* drivers, milling about the dusty Vientiane bus station like a swarm of ants on the outskirts of a picnic blanket.

"Go see Nok. I'll catch you at home," he called over his shoulder.

"Hey, Somchai!" I called out. "Here's some money. For the doctor and stuff. I hope it's enough." I handed him a fat wad of dry *kip* I had kept tucked in my backpack. He nodded.

❧

There's nothing like nerves to clear away a hangover. My heart hammered up in my temples. Would she change her mind about me?

Turns out I didn't have to worry about it just then. The door to the massage house was locked. A torn piece of white paper with swirly Lao characters was taped to the window explaining why. I couldn't read it. I balanced on one crutch so I could knock on the door. No answer. Why would it be closed on a Sunday afternoon? Weekends were their busiest times. Nana would never miss out on the business. Something wasn't right.

A rusty pickup truck rounded the corner filled with a mob of teenagers, their buckets of water and massive water guns barely visible through the spray. So that was it.

Closed for Lao New Year. My stomach sank. It was another day until the holiday ended.

Damn, I thought, resting my forehead against the massage house door. I felt my shoulders tense up again. I wanted to see her now. I knew what to do to make things right again.

HELP

Seng

Seng thought he would take a shortcut to the main road. He would flag down the first vehicle he saw and ask the driver to get a doctor. If only they were in America and he could call an ambulance. If only he owned a cellphone. This was all his fault. The *Pi Mai* moon wasn't helping him to see anything. There was so much darkness. Was he going the right way? He shook his head violently, trying to clear away the fog from his mind. None of this could really be happening. Nok was going to be okay. She probably just had a bad cut on the back of her head. She was going to be — he stopped short. He couldn't hear cars or motorbikes. This couldn't be the right way. He turned around. He couldn't see a thing. He suddenly noticed that his ankle was throbbing. He must have twisted it or something when he fell off the bike. His heart hammered inside his body and his mouth was dry. He was panting like a wild animal.

The smell of earth and bush was all around. He tried to block it out. The only smell he wanted was hers. He was afraid something else would replace it. He didn't want to forget. He plugged his nose with his fingers but then he couldn't run as quickly. If only he wasn't so fat, then he could run faster. This was wrong, all wrong. He wanted to start from the beginning. When all five of them were together — his entire family. How he had failed Meh now! He had killed her baby. Killed his sister! He *was* a wild animal. But no, he was wrong. He couldn't afford to think this way. Nok was going to survive. She was too strong not to. Besides, he couldn't live without her. If she was dead he would be as well.

Sweat poured down his forehead. He was so afraid. Where was he? He still couldn't hear the sounds of a road.

"Someone help me!" he screamed. "Help!"

All of a sudden he tripped over a thick tree root. He felt his body go down, his head slam against something hard. And then there was nothing. Absolutely nothing.

There would never be anything again.

Not without her.

HALO

Seng

Seng woke with a start, disoriented and confused. He sat up and looked around. Dawn in the forest. Through the black silhouette of trees he could see the blue-gray of a lightening sky. His tongue was like sandpaper. His head throbbed. He felt the back of it and through his thick, damp hair he found a large goose egg. Birds noisily announced the beginning of a new day, a new year. With a flash of pain the memory came back.

"Nok!" he whispered and stood up too quickly. He stumbled, feeling dizzy and weak. He looked all around but could only see the trunks of trees. He turned and limped through the woods as quickly as he could.

When he came to the edge of the road where he had left her he saw the massive truck. The driver was standing beside it with white gauze taped on his forehead. He held on to the truck's door handle as he talked to a man dressed in the beige uniform of the investigative police. The officer nodded, listening intently, and writing furiously in a notebook. Seng walked closer toward them. Hopefully, he scanned the scene for his sister, but she was gone. Only the stain of her halo remained on the dirt road. He was relieved to see the men and was about to step out of the roadside brush and call out to them when the driver slammed his hand violently onto the side of the truck. Seng froze in his place in the bushes.

"That son of a bitch! A girl is dead because of him. And now her death will be part of my karma. If I see him I will kill him myself. Such a beautiful, young girl. Dead! And he left her alone! He took off. He deserves to die, that driver. He deserves to die." The driver slammed his hand against the truck again.

"He very well might," said the officer said in a way that was almost hopeful.

The truck driver stopped his outburst and looked up. "What do you mean?"

"The government is looking to make an example of someone. No one takes the drunk driving laws seriously. If this guy is charged with manslaughter everyone will take notice. Especially if he gets the death penalty for it."

"The death penalty? For driving drunk?"

"For driving drunk and killing someone," the officer said.

"But how do you know he was drunk?"

"You said he was driving on the wrong side of the road, weaving back and forth?"

"Yeah, that's right."

"Classic sign."

"Mr. Phon, where's the girl now? I need to see her. She died because of me."

"Based on your statements you did nothing wrong."

"If I hadn't been driving on this road ..." The truck driver's voice trailed off as he looked at his feet. Seng could see him wiping his eyes.

"She's at the morgue," Officer Phon continued.

Seng's heart plummeted and he closed his eyes, stunned. He couldn't move. *This isn't real*, he said over and over again in his head. *This can't be real.*

"We found a business card on her body," the officer continued. "She worked at one of the massage houses. Her co-worker identified her."

"Not her family?"

"Apparently there is a brother, but we can't find him. The co-worker said there is a boyfriend, too. A *falang*. She said they were both supposed to be at the party."

Seng fell to his knees. The officer suddenly turned in his direction, peering carefully into the bush, as if he had heard something, but then he shrugged, seeming to dismiss the idea. Seng buried his face into his trembling hands. Then he covered his mouth to stifle his sobs.

Finally he heard the engine of the officer's motorbike starting. He turned to look up and could see the truck driver crouched over the place where Nok had fell, his head bent. Seng stood up slowly, as quietly as he could. He wanted someone with whom to share his grief. He would go to the man and they could weep together. Seng took a step forward, but then thought again. He turned around and darted back into the deep bush.

BLUR

Cam

Julia had freaked out about my injuries from the fall in the cave.

"They sewed you up without anesthetic? How do you know the needle was clean? Somchai should have contacted me."

"Somchai was perfect. I'm glad he was there instead of you."

"We need to take you to the international clinic as soon as Lao New Year is over. I'm making an appointment."

But the day after Lao New Year I woke up before Julia and painstakingly biked past farmers ushering their water buffalos through fields. My slow pace was making me feel like a water buffalo. I didn't care about my stupid ankle. I only wanted to see Nok. That's what I needed to feel better. I was so anxious to get to Fa Ngum Massage, but my ankle kept sending twinges of pain up my leg, even though the doctor in Vang Vieng said I could begin putting weight on it after a few days. It was taking me so long to get there. I was desperate to find the door to the massage house propped open just as it always was in the mornings to allow the cooler air in. I arrived at last, breathless and sore, and was totally relieved when I saw Nana unlocking the front door. I had driven by five times during the last day of Lao New Year, but the door was always locked. I waved at Nana and attempted a smile. She didn't smile back. The corners of my mouth shook with nerves. I was definitely not playing it cool.

Nana stopped fiddling with her keys and searched my eyes apprehensively. Was she afraid that I was still angry? She didn't understand English, but before I could put the Lao words together to apologize she launched into a staccato monologue. She was frantic. I tried to follow, but she was speaking so quickly. Nerves stymied my brain. Her chubby hands were waving all over the place, her eyes looked terrified. I was making out some words: terrible, New Year, Nok's gone, not here. But as she rattled on, and the searing sun began to prick at my neck, my impatience grew and made it even more difficult for me to understand. Soon Nana's story became so twisted and disjointed in my head that I pretended I understood and quickly left in a haze of frustration. I needed Somchai.

I biked to the plastics factory near our village where he said he was going to look for a job. He wasn't going to even bother trying to go to school this semester. My mind was so frantic I didn't notice the rain. After months of living in a dry sauna the few drops promised that the wet season would finally come. I should have been doing pop-a-wheelies for joy. Instead I was freaking out. Had something awful happened? Or was Nana giving me a piece of her mind for losing it on her friend?

I skidded my bike into the plastics factory courtyard and spotted Somchai standing in a long line of men, their hands turned upwards towards the sky, trying to feel the relief of raindrops on their sweaty palms. He saw me and waved me over.

"Rain!" he said with a laugh, his bright face turned up to the darkening sky. Then he turned to look at me. "Hey," he said, "you shouldn't be biking yet."

"Somchai, you've got to come with me."

"What? Why aren't you at school?"

"It's Nok. I think something bad has happened. She's not at the massage house. I need you to translate."

It was only after Somchai doubled me on the back of my bike and we were halfway to the massage house that I realized he had left his place in line for me.

When we got back to Fa Ngum Massage, the other masseuses scattered as soon as they saw me. One of them called for Nana. Nana walked down the stairs to the front desk of the massage house and held her hand up to her heart as she began to chatter anxiously to Somchai. My gut wrenched. I didn't understand a thing. I watched Somchai's face fall. I was so afraid and powerless, standing there, stupid, yet at the same time knowing that things would never be the same again. All I could do was wait. It seemed like they were talking for an eternity. Finally, Somchai turned to me.

"Brother," he said, and I could tell by the softening of his voice that it was really bad. He paused, trying to find the right way to tell me.

"I'm so sorry." He swallowed. "She is gone. Nok died. I'm sorry, Cam." His gentle face, the empty room, Nana's sad eyes watching me closely — it all blurred at the edges. I couldn't see right. I couldn't have heard right. Somchai wrapped his strong, sinewy arms around me.

"No, it's a mistake," I said. "It can't be."

Somchai hugged me tighter.

"How?" I looked up from Somchai's shoulder, tears like monsoon rain down my cheeks. Nana just shook her head. My voice squeaked. "Somchai? How?"

"It was a motorbike accident, brother," he said gently. "After a New Year party."

I hung my head. The party I was supposed to go to.

"Who was driving?" I wanted someone to be angry at. Someone to blame.

"Nana doesn't know, Cam. She said there is a police investigation underway."

"What do you mean?"

"Nok was alone, by the bike. The police said she fell off the back. The driver has disappeared."

It had to be a mistake. It couldn't have really happened. I must still be in a fog from Vang Vieng. Once it cleared, everything would be back to normal. I just had to wait it out. In a trance, I let Somchai double me on my bike back to our village. My body felt so heavy I could barely move it. I slumped up against his back as his feet pedalled up and down, up and down.

Everything was in slow motion. I watched, as if I were watching images on a TV screen, as Somchai prayed at a tiny replica of a temple perched on a white post in front of his home. A spirit house, he called it. The spirit house — white and red with an ornate roof curving up to a sharp, golden point — looked like a miniature version of the temple where Nok had taken me. I had noticed that most Lao homes had one in front. The tall palm trees of our village rustled nervously. Somchai lit a stick of incense and the fragrant smoke drifted languidly around us. He placed it by the small front door. I saw him close his dark eyes, place his hands in prayer at his forehead, and mouth a prayer. I heard the air eddy about his lips as he chanted wordlessly. Bad spirits out, good spirits in. I staggered. Nothing felt real.

ALIBI

Seng

Seng crouched in the shadows, tossing pebbles at the shutters of Khamdeng's window. After hearing what the investigative officer told the truck driver, he had spent the day in the bush, drinking water from a trickling stream to replenish his tears. Nok was gone. Dead. There would be no university, no *falang* love, no hope. He had never felt so alone or so terrified. The death penalty? He would have gladly died in the accident instead of Nok. In fact it should have been him. But it was another thing to have his life taken by the government. He shook his head. He couldn't believe he was even thinking about these things. He'd give anything to worry about something as stupid as how many plastic combs he could sell.

It was as if he existed outside of himself now. It was like he could watch himself in the forest, as he bent to splash his face with water from the stream or bury his hands in his face. He watched his chest heave as he wept. Saw himself take a piss and sit staring at the ground, completely lost. He had to go to her, to retrieve her body. Bury her properly.

The morning had slipped into noon before he remembered Khamdeng. The motorbike belonged to him. Officer Phon would have wasted no time tracking him down. Seng had heard rumours about investigative police beating people up in order get them to talk. What would they do to his friend? His nerves shook as he wrung his hands together, desperate for night to fall so he could get to his friend in secrecy. The late afternoon seemed to last for days. Now, finally, Khamdeng called out through closed shutters.

"Who's there?"

"Brother, it's me."

Khamdeng slowly opened the shutters. In the moonlight Seng could see his puffy, black eye. Seng gasped.

"They were here," Seng said, hanging his head. Khamdeng held a finger up to his mouth to shush Seng. He motioned for Seng to go around to the front of the house. Seng's blood raced through his veins as he skulked to Khamdeng's front door. His friend let him in and they knelt together, whispering, in a dark corner of Khamdeng's home. The moonlight seeped in through the slats of a shutter, eerily illuminating the room and Khamdeng's face.

"You can't stay here. They are looking for you. That Officer Phon is on a mission. He wants to make an example out of you," Khamdeng whispered frantically.

"What did they do to you?"

Khamdeng didn't answer. "It's not safe for you in Vientiane, Seng. You have to leave."

"Khamdeng, what did they do?"

His friend looked into his lap. After a while he began to talk. "There were three of them. It didn't matter what they did to me. I wasn't going to tell them anything. They took turns, but my mouth wouldn't move. I wouldn't say your name, Seng."

Seng began to scratch the back of his head furiously. "You should have just said it! I deserve everything I get, but I am not good enough for your loyalty." His voice quivered.

Khamdeng was quiet for a long time. Then he swallowed. "It was when they turned on Meh, Seng. Two of them did. I said it then. So they would stop."

Seng felt his heart pop. He whispered in a shaky voice, "Your *meh* — is she okay?"

Khamdeng nodded.

"No one should suffer but me," Seng said. "You did the right thing, giving them my name."

"But it wasn't your name, brother."

Seng met his eyes. He couldn't speak.

"What do you mean?" he finally asked.

Khamdeng fingered the bottom of his T-shirt. "I said it was the *falang*. The Canadian boyfriend."

"But —" Seng was stunned.

"What else could I do? I don't even know his name, so they don't have his details. All they know was that it was a foreigner."

"But he wasn't there! He's innocent!"

"Shh, keep your voice down." Khamdeng swallowed. "I know, I can't stop thinking about that. But it's my duty to protect my family and friends. I didn't know what else to do."

"I'm going to turn myself in right now."

"No! If you do you will be charged with manslaughter. That's what the officer said. They want to prove to the world they can get tough on drunk driving — apparently the tourists were getting worried about it. They will know that I lied. We will both be dead."

"But what if they find the *falang*?"

"He's a foreigner. They will take it easy on him. Besides, his government will bail him out. They'll have all kinds of fancy legal people to prove that he's innocent. He'll be safe in Canada in no time."

"This is so wrong. It's all wrong, Khamdeng. We can't do this."

"Seng, hasn't your family lost enough? They took your parents. Your *pa* and *meh* wouldn't want them to take you, too."

Seng hugged himself and then collapsed forward in his cross-legged position. His forehead met the floor. Soon it was slick with tears and snot.

They sat silent for a long time. His mind raced. He couldn't do this. Finally Khamdeng said, "I sent an e-mail to your big sister. I didn't say anything in it that would blame you — they check e-mail, you know. I just told her that Nok died. She is on her way."

"What?" Seng sat up. He wiped his face with the back of his hand.

"Vong. She's coming — to Vientiane."

"No! I don't want her here."

"Seng, she needed to know. About Nok. Maybe she can help you."

"No, she's never helped me."

"She took care of you after your parents were taken! She was only a teenager herself."

"And then she left us."

"After you were grown. Look, Seng, she's your family. Aren't you always missing having your family together? She needs to know."

"I don't want her to know how I have failed," Seng said, looking down. "I don't want her to know what I've done!"

Just then they heard a rustling sound coming from deeper inside Khamdeng's house.

"Seng, you have to go now. I don't want anyone to know you were here. In case someone asks them."

Seng nodded and crept as quietly as he could outside. He had no clue where to go or what to do next.

FREEDOM HEAD-ON

Cam

I stayed in bed for days after I found out about Nok's death. I didn't speak to anyone, not even Somchai. But he had told Julia everything. Now she was knocking on my door hourly, asking me if I needed anything, leaving plates of macaroni and cheese or vanilla pudding on the floor by my bed. My childhood favourites. She must have cooked them herself. You can't buy those things in Vientiane.

"I'm sorry, Cameron. About Nok," she said uncomfortably, standing at my bedroom door. "I had no idea." She apparently stayed home from work; through the sound of the harsh rain viciously hammering our tin roof, I heard her as she moved around the house. She came to my room regularly, to bring me food or tell me that Somchai was at the door.

"Tell him to go away." I knew he would make me feel better and I didn't want to feel better yet. I had been like a plant in the Canadian spring, waking up from a long, harsh winter and daring to poke its tender head out of the soil, only to be frozen to death by a cruel and unexpected frost.

"Cam, I think you should get up. Go outside for a little bit. Get some fresh air."

I rolled over to my other side so she couldn't see my face. The next day she tried again.

"Cam, don't you think you'd feel better if you got up?"

I was annoyed by her intrusions into my isolation.

"You know what? This is your entire fault," I said. Suddenly I wanted to tear into her. I had been craving someone to blame. It felt good to find a target. Of course it was her fault.

"If it wasn't for you I would have never met her. I wouldn't be in this stupid country!" I was screaming now, like a little kid, with snot and tears streaming down my face. "I hate you more now than when I was a kid. Why don't you just fuck off!"

She sat at the edge of my bed, like she didn't know what to do. She had this sympathetic, compassionate look on her face. For a second I saw how pathetic I must seem in her eyes. It made me sick. She wouldn't leave so finally I stood up, dizzy and weak. I grabbed some clothes and tromped through the house, slamming the front door shut.

I stepped out into the humid evening, woozy and mad. A red sunset smeared across the sky like a wound. It was my first time out in the world since I found out about Nok's death. I climbed onto my bike and my ankle twinged as a reminder of my fall in the cave. A reminder of a time before all of this. When Nok was alive and we were eager to see what would happen. Now there was no future. I tried to pedal fast, but soon I felt winded and weak.

"*Oi!*" an old woman on a bicycle yelled as she veered to avoid hitting me.

I was out of it. Like an alien, hovering above everything, observing as if I couldn't be seen.

I slowed down, pedalling slowly through the smoky evening air to *Patuxai*, the Victory monument — Laos's version of Paris's Arc de Triomphe. Carved into the mushroom-coloured sides of the mammoth, concrete arch were mythical Buddhist creatures, part human, part bird, with round breasts and pointed, elaborate head-dresses. *Bird* — it was the meaning of Nok's name.

Exhaust, thick in the muggy twilight, spewed out of the hundreds of motorbikes, aging Russian cars, and rusty pickup trucks circling the arch's roundabout. Coconut trees, stooped like mourning people, stood along the stone road that led underneath the monument. I noticed a man pacing the coral-coloured road, his dark brown face glistening with sweat as he clutched a main cord that had several tiny, square, wicker cages tied to it. I heard the peeping and twittering of small birds and immediately knew what he was selling. Merit birds.

I cycled over to the man; he nodded at me and pointed to the panicky plovers, asking if I wanted to buy. I looked at the birds, frantic and fragile, trapped and helpless, in their cages. I wondered where they were from. Probably nowhere near the busy Patuxai traffic circle. Wouldn't it have been better to leave the birds to their freedom in the first place?

"I'll take them all," I said.

The man looked up, surprised.

"*Muht?*"

"Yeah, all." I reached into the pocket of my shorts to pull out a limp wad of dirty *kip* bills. I passed the money to the man and he looked pleased with himself as he counted each bill. He watched me as I propped my bike against the victory arch, took the chain of cages from his hand, and made my way to a stretch of green grass. There were about ten cages tied to the main cord. The birds fluttered anxiously in their makeshift jails. In some, two birds were stuffed inside.

My blundering fingers fiddled with the little wicker loop that closed the first cage shut. The bird trapped inside quivered. I was so anxious to free him that it was making me clumsy with the lock. Impatient, I yanked on it, but it made the bird more terrified. I had to slow down. Finally, I was able to undo the loop and open the door. I could almost feel the bird's tiny heart pounding as he whirred past me to freedom. By now the sky was dusky grey and it was difficult to see where he flew, but I caught sight of his silhouette soaring past the beam of a light sitting on top of the arch. I wondered if he would be able to find his way home.

The other birds twittered impatiently, as if they knew they would be next. Urged by their restlessness, I quickly undid more cages. Flapping wings buzzed in my ears and I saw the birds gather and swoop in the twilight. With each bird released I felt lighter. Perhaps this vicarious feeling of freedom was why people paid money to let them go. Feeling calmer, I freed another, and another.

Then I came to the last trembling bird. I loosened the loop locking his cage and the brown plover peered out of the open door, dumbfounded by his new freedom. He looked from side to side, but stayed perched on the edge of the cage door.

"Go!" I urged him. "Get out of here."

But the bird stayed — so used to the cage, and so fearful of the unknown.

"Fly!" I yelled, annoyed by his stupidity.

I jiggled the cage a bit. Finally he peered from side to side one last time and then lifted off and up into the boundless night sky. I watched his little outstretched wings as he soared up near the top of the arch, claiming his victory, but then suddenly he swooped back down near the traffic circle. Over again he swept up and floated back down, as if on some kind of aviary roller coaster. He was making me nervous, the way he glided so close to the evening traffic. Why wouldn't he just fly away to the clump of trees on the other side of the road? I heard the flutter of his wings as he swooped past me. It was almost as if he still had one eye on the cage, which now lay open and useless on the ground.

"You're free! Just go!" I swatted my hand in his direction.

I strained my eyes to follow him in the darkening sky. I'd momentarily lose sight of him and worry until I spotted him again, flitting under the arch.

I followed him with my eyes for some time. I decided a captor probably really makes merit when he no longer captures. I caught a glimpse of the merit bird seller, slurping noodles at a street vendor's cart. I knew it was my *kip* that had bought his dinner. The night settled in and the vendors lit their kerosene lanterns. I saw steam rising in the lamplight from the soy milk and spring rolls they sold. I sat down in the grass, my head turned up to the sky. I saw my bird make another dramatic swoop up into the air, only to cast himself back down into the headlights of oncoming traffic. The motorcyclist didn't even realize she had hit him.

I ran to the edge of the busy road and stood on the perimeter, as close to his shattered body as I could get. Motorbikes and cars whizzed by, oblivious to his death. In the light from the arch I could make out my bird's flattened body, his brown feathers flapping lifelessly every time a vehicle zoomed past.

I sat on my knees, right on the edge of the hectic roundabout, and didn't want to ever get up again.

REUNITED

Seng

Seng anxiously packed a bag in the darkness of his and Nok's deserted house. He was trying to think of what he might need, but the problem was he didn't know what he was going to do. He couldn't live in the bush forever. He also couldn't live with the guilt of the foreigner suffering. Nok said his name was Cam. It meant gold.

He was so hysterical that his movements were clumsy. He had to get out of there before Vong arrived. He didn't want her to know what he had done. He couldn't bear to see the pain on her face. The pain that he had put there. He had traded his whole life, everything that mattered to him, for a drunk buzz. Talk about an idiot.

He kept knocking things over. A Beerlao calendar with *Sabaidee Pi Mai* written on it in bright, happy characters fell to the ground in a shadowy corner. He jumped. He looked up at the black-and-white pictures of their parents. Small mantles sat underneath each photo for offerings to their spirits — incense, sticks of brown *longan* fruit, and cones fashioned from browning banana leaves and wilting marigolds. Just three days ago Nok had put the offerings there for Lao New Year. Just three days ago she had stood there, radiantly alive.

"What should I do now?" he whispered to his mother's picture. "How I have failed you!" He stuffed his mother's picture into his bag. He said a silent prayer that Nok would be with her now.

He was zipping his bag shut when he heard a noise outside, like a *tuk-tuk* trundling away from the front of the house. His heart beat frantically, like a bird just caught and stuffed into a cage. He tried to peer between the slats of the closed shutter. In the darkness he could make out a silhouette. Someone was standing in the driveway. He would escape out the back door and into the thicket of banana trees behind their house. They would never catch him. They had taken away too much.

"Seng?" he heard a woman call. He froze in his tracks. It had been three years, but she sounded exactly the same. It was as if he were a kid again and she was calling him inside for supper.

Now she was at the door, letting herself in. She still had a key. She walked in and they faced each other, two black shadows in the night.

"Vong."

"Brother," she said and began to weep. He could hear her sniffling and faltering breath. "I am so sorry, my brother."

He couldn't help but go to her then. As he walked closer he could see that she was fatter now. She looked up and in the moonlight he could see laughing wrinkles around her eyes, like cracks in mud during the dry season. She looked older than she should.

He fell into her arms and despite all of his fears about her judgments and pain, it felt good to feel the warm embrace of family.

"Sister, you are home."

FUGITIVE

Seng

When Seng finished telling the story of the accident,
Vong remained silent. She looked like she was fighting
against a tsunami of rage and grief. He scratched the
back of his neck nervously. Finally, after some time of
sitting in silence on the floor beside him, she said she was
exhausted. She patted Seng's hand. He wanted to know
what she was thinking. Did she hate him? She didn't even
know the worst of what he had done yet. He didn't tell
her about leaving Nok alone on the road.

"I need to sleep now," she said.

She stumbled to a plastic woven mat on the floor;
it was only after she was under the green mosquito net
and Seng had turned out the light that he saw her curl
into a fetal position in the moonlight and begin to heave
silently. He wanted to go to her. He was surprised at
how her presence comforted him. He did feel better
with her around, but he couldn't drag her into his plan.
He needed her to fall asleep so he could leave right away.

Night sounds surrounded the small house — howling

dogs and belching bullfrogs. They would cover the sound of his footsteps. He would slip out of the house silently, leaving another sister alone. She would understand. After all, she was the first to leave.

He turned and went to search for his bag in the darkness. Suddenly she stood up and flicked on the light.

"Little brother?" she asked tenderly.

Seng turned around, shocked. He didn't know what to say. They stood there, facing each other, blinking as their eyes adjusted to the bright light. Suddenly he let his bag drop onto the floor.

"I'm so afraid, *euaigh*," he said in a small voice.

Euaigh. Big sister. She knelt beside him and sniffed at the top of his head in a Lao-style kiss. It reminded him of their mom; how she would tiptoe in the night around the space where they slept on the floor. She would kneel so quietly beside them, convinced they were sound asleep, and sniff each one of their heads or stroke their cheeks, mouthing prayers for them.

In Vong's arms, Seng's sturdy body shook. His head was slick with sweat.

"The police will come for me. They are starting to crack down on drunk driving now, like in your country. They will make an example of me."

"What did the police say after the accident?"

"I don't know, *euaigh*. I didn't see them. I ran away."

"You did what?"

"I ran. Into the bush. I wanted to find help, but I couldn't. I just came back to the house tonight to gather some things. Then I'm leaving." He was scratching the back of his head like a madman.

"Seng, how could you —"

"I know, I deserve to be in jail. But it would break Nok's heart. All of our dreams — evaporated. Too much has been taken away from our family. Too much," he hung his head and sobbed. "I'm not going into jail."

Vong's mouth hung open.

"But where ... where is her body?" she asked. The words sounded so toxic, like poison entering his body through his ears.

"She was at the morgue. Nana came and got her. Gave her a proper funeral. I watched it from the bushes."

"What? Damn it, Seng! There has already been a funeral?"

"I'm sorry, sister. Khamdeng said you were coming, but I didn't know when. You never answered my e-mails." He hadn't wanted to bring it up so soon, but it just slipped out. He was having a hard time holding things together.

He watched Vong swallow hard.

"They're trying to find me," he continued. "They already questioned Khamdeng."

Vong looked around the room, as if she was searching for an answer in the blackness.

"You have to come with me," she blurted out.

"To America?"

"Seng, I don't live in America."

"What?"

For three years he hadn't even know what country she lived in? He was that much of a dimwit?

"I live in Canada."

The word *Canada* was like a slap on his cheek. He hadn't told her about what Khamdeng said to the police. He was trying to push the *falang* far out of his mind. He stood there, eyes searching his sister. He was suddenly struck by how much they looked alike. Their pudgy, stocky bodies, Meh's big round eyes and face. How could it be that they were so far apart now?

"Turn the light off, *euaigh*. I don't want anyone to know we are here."

In hushed voices, Seng and Vong made their plan.

WORSE

Cam

Somchai woke me from a restless sleep early one Monday morning. He yanked the thin cover off me.

"How'd you get in here?" I croaked. I hadn't said a word to anyone since three days ago at the victory monument.

"Julia finally let me in, in spite of the fact that you've been telling her not to. I can't believe you're still in bed. Come on, this is enough. She died — you didn't. Your mom told me you haven't been back to school yet." He dug through my drawers, threw some clothes on my bed. "You're going to school."

I rolled over and pulled the covers over my head.

"Golden brother, I would love to go to school for you, believe me, but I have to get to my job. My uncle got one for me at the Vietnamese sandwich shop. Chopping vegetables. They're expecting me. Get up."

I stood up. Somchai gave me a light-hearted shove.

"That's better. See you after work." I heard our rusty front gate slam shut behind him.

My head throbbed as I trudged through the school hallway. I could hear the noise of homeroom as I got closer. Olivia, the New Zealand girl I'd met at the beginning of the semester, babbled about a weekend trip to Nam Ngum. I heard another group talk about where they were going for lunch. I dreaded opening the door, entering the bright classroom. They all seemed so naive. Their lives were so simple.

I finally opened it and the conversations screeched to a halt as swiftly as a head-on collision. The room was silent except for the sound of the rickety ceiling fan rotating overhead. I conspicuously found my desk. Why was everyone looking at me? Thankfully, Mr. Rose finally entered the humid room and broke the silence as he dropped textbooks on his desk with a clunk. He nodded curtly at me.

"Long time no see." His eyes searched me, concerned.

I couldn't focus on anything during class. Mr. Rose finished his lesson and we worked on some algebra problems by ourselves. I could hear the scratching of pencils and see my classmates, their heads bent earnestly over their work. I stared down at the blank notebook in front of me. I couldn't think about anything but Nok. Who was driving her on that night? My mind was a jumble. Maybe it was all some kind of joke. Maybe I would run into her somewhere. I imagined how she would smile and take my hand.

"Come on, Cam," she would say, all glistening and full of life. "Let's go for a walk."

Mr. Rose interrupted my thoughts. I could sense him standing over my desk.

"We've got to talk," he whispered. "Come to my office after school. I'll arrange for a meeting." He sounded too serious.

Had he heard about Nok? Or was he mad because I'd missed so much school. It couldn't still be about the basketball fight, could it? So much had happened since then, it seemed like lifetimes ago. I had almost forgotten about the Thai guard.

Turns out no one else had.

"I hear he has brain damage," my German teammate told me in between periods. "I thought that's why you haven't bothered to show up at school."

Saliva thickened in my mouth. I tried to swallow. During my days in bed I had wondered how life could possibly be worse. Now I knew. I couldn't wait until after school to talk to Mr. Rose. I had to see him now. It felt like everyone's eyes were on me as I speed-walked through the hallway to his office. I saw girls beside their lockers, whispering to each other. Anthony, our team goon, caught up to me and pushed the back of my shoulder.

"Way to go." He laughed stupidly. "You really gave it to him."

I finally made it to Mr. Rose's office, but he wasn't there. I'd have to wait. I went outside to the school track. A burst of monsoon rain had started, turning the track into a red mud bath. I didn't care. I ran it anyway. I ran as fast as I could, around and around again. Crimson earth splattered up my calves, squished in the Nike knock-offs Julia had bought me at the Morning Market, and bled onto my shirt like I had been shot in the heart. I could taste earth in my mouth and feel its grit in my teeth. The mud squelched as my feet pounded against it. A sharp stitch stretched across my side. I ignored it and sprinted faster and faster until finally I doubled over, heaving and breathless.

ESCAPE

Seng

Seng couldn't leave Laos legally. Despite the country's slip-shod rules and sleepy border guards, he would definitely be caught. Mother Water would have to save them. They'd travel across the Mekong River and into Thailand on the other side. Vong said she heard of riverbanks farther south of the city so completely covered in brush that no one would see them descend into the wide river. A villager there would take them on a fishing boat.

"Who told you about that?" Seng asked.

"Someone I know." She shrugged uncomfortably. He was beginning to wonder if he knew this sister at all.

"But what about when we reach the other side? Won't the Thais spot us?" He hoped his voice wasn't giving away how nervous he felt. He didn't want Vong to know how dependent he felt on her right now. Another sister bailing him out.

"We'll take our chances. They don't patrol the entire riverbank."

From Nong Khai they'd take the train to Bangkok.

From there, they'd have to see about Canada. Vong said she had a little savings they could live off for a while.

The next night, they didn't speak as they moved along Vientiane's shadowy edges. The moonless sky was a gift from the spirits, cloaking them in darkness so complete they could barely see each other. Seng was edgy — jumping at the sound of a matted village dog sniffing out a companion in the night, or at the spark of a motorbike engine starting on a dark street. But Vong looked focused. They walked soundlessly throughout the long night. Seng flinched at the gravely call of a bulbul bird. Dawn would soon come. He thought he could smell the smoke of a villager's morning fire.

"She said it was somewhere along here," Vong whispered absentmindedly to herself.

"Who did?" Seng asked. She ignored him. What else had this sister kept from him? He still couldn't believe all this time he'd thought she was in America.

She pulled back razor-sharp branches from their faces as they skulked through dense brush towards the Mekong. He heard the sound of water rushing. The great river heaved forward through the humid night. Mosquitoes swarmed them. Vong reached up to slap a mosquito feasting on the back of her sweaty neck. She let go of a branch too soon and it flung behind her viciously to catch Seng in the cheekbone. He felt a trickle of blood ooze down his face. The weight of their actions struck him, as an angry hand strikes a cheek. What the hell was she thinking? Why was he following her so dumbly? But then the smell of a cigarette met his nose. Someone was nearby.

"We're here," Vong whispered. She cleared back the last

swatch of brush to reveal an elderly man crouched along the dark riverbank, puffing peacefully on a hand-rolled cigarette.

"Good evening, my child," he spoke to Vong in a soft, shaky voice. "To Thailand?" He nodded toward the Mekong, shimmering like an oil slick in the night. The old man was shirtless, wearing nothing but dirty white shorts on his thin body. His ribs stuck out and his gentle smile was toothless. In the shadowy moonlight Seng could see his cropped, white hair, thin and stark on his dark brown head.

Vong nodded and placed a massive wad of bills in his old, gnarled hands.

"Quickly, sir," she whispered. "Morning is coming."

The fugitives boarded a worn, long-tail boat and the old man pushed a bamboo stick into the riverbank, casting them out into the deep, dark water. Seng was stunned. He had lived in this city for most of his life and didn't know that, as he slept, people did this kind of thing. Escaped crimes. How many Lao people had this man rowed across to Thai shores? How did Vong know about him? He thought better about asking his questions. He had some brains left. Silence was the only thing that could serve them at the moment.

He thought of Nok and wondered where Nana had put her ashes. He listened to the old wooden boat slide through the water and chanted a thousand silent prayers for the dead and the living. He wasn't sure which category he fit into at the moment. Was there an almost-dead category?

The bank on the other side loomed imminent and black in the night. But there were no Thai police walking up and down with flashlights or dogs barking ferociously to announce their arrival. Just an elderly woman in a fading *sin* beckoning them toward her. Seng's eyes met Vong's.

"A Lao sister," the old man explained. "She lives in Thailand now. Follow her. She will show you where to go."

Vong grasped their elderly captain's bony hands in hers.

"You have a good heart," she whispered.

"Be safe, my child."

Suddenly, Seng slipped as he stepped out of the boat, hurtling into the water. His stocky body met the dark river with a loud splash. He felt the cool water envelop his body. He couldn't swim. He kicked and flailed violently. He didn't know which way was up. A pressure grew in his head as he felt water filling his ears and nose. Bubbles were all around, but the longer he was underwater the slower they became. Soon he could only see a shimmer of blackness and moonlight. His body began to feel so heavy and his pounding heart gave way to a strange calmness. *This might be the way to escape*, he thought, and stopped kicking so hard. Now he understood how the dead could be grateful. He let his body go limp. He wondered if this is how it felt in the womb. When there was no space between him and his mother, when he existed between earth and the otherworld.

Suddenly he felt a sharp poke on the top of his head, as if someone was poking him with a stick.

No, he thought. *Let me be.*

But the stick wouldn't stop its probing. It annoyed Seng and he batted at it with his hand, but the stick persisted. He grabbed on to it tightly, hoping to pull it from the hands of the person on the other end, but instead he was dragged up out of the river, coughing and gasping, his loud panting floating along the river, on the edge where air meets water. He looked up to see Vong leaning over the edge of the old man's long-tail boat, reeling him in like a fish. He could see the relief in her eyes as she dragged him to the boat's edge and she and the man hoisted him onto the deck. She had saved his life. He didn't feel so grateful anymore.

He couldn't stand upright. He felt like his knees were going to double beneath him. He shook his head, but the water in his ears wouldn't budge, nor would the strange feeling of disappointment.

Vong hugged him fiercely and then took a hand towel from her backpack to dry her brother's shivering body. He wasn't cold in the hot night. He was shaking with fear. She looked in her brother's eyes and placed both hands on his shoulders, attempting to steady him.

"It's going to be okay, Seng."

Seng doubted that very much, but he followed her off the boat, as a dog follows its owner.

The old woman was waiting silently at the forest's edge. Seng's wet flip-flops flapped too noisily against his feet as they followed her wordlessly through dense Thai brush. Finally the sky lightened above them and swallows and fairy-bluebirds announced dawn's arrival. Seng's pulse began to slow to a normal pace.

"We are coming to the end of the forest now. You may cross over the farmer's field at the forest's edge in safety. Beyond the field is a market, where you can find some breakfast." The old woman had clearly explained this many times before.

"Why do you do this?" Vong asked.

The old woman smiled. "I was a dancer in the king's court."

They immediately knew how the woman's story ended. All of the dancers were stolen away. They were interned in political re-education camps. Somehow, this woman must have escaped or been freed. Seng wondered if perhaps she had known their mother. In another situation he would have asked. Right now he didn't know if he could even find his voice.

The woman watched them from the lush foliage as they walked along the perimeter of the farmer's green rice paddy. It wasn't until they were alone in the bustling, rural Thai market that Seng dared to speak.

"Now what?" he asked.

MANSLAUGHTER

Cam

Mr. Rose finally answered my pounding on his door. I walked into his office and stopped short. Julia was there, sitting with her long, pale legs crossed in one of the wooden chairs across from Mr. Rose's desk.

"What are you doing here?" I asked.

"Cam, you should have told me about the basketball fight," she said gently. I could tell she was taking it easy on me because of Nok.

"You would have known about it if you'd come."

She looked towards the window and inhaled audibly.

"Cam, Ms. White, I've called you in here because the police want to investigate," Mr. Rose said, a look of pity softening his stern eyes.

Julia leaned forward in her seat. "What?"

I was stunned. I sat silent. I couldn't take anymore. Fuck Julia for bringing me to this country.

"I've been handling it up until now," Mr. Rose explained. "I thought the other coach and I would be able to work it out, but the guard's family wants to press charges."

"But I didn't mean to hurt him so badly." My voice sounded small and muted, like it wasn't coming from me. My throat was as dry as Vientiane before the rains, but my palms were monsoon-damp. "He started it. Fights happen in basketball all the time."

"Cam, he had two fractured vertebrae in his neck, a major concussion, vertebral ligament damage, and facial wounds. That does not happen in basketball all the time." Mr. Rose fiddled nervously with a paper clip on his desk.

I stared at the red mud dribbling down my shins like blood. I wished I had run away instead of racing around the track like a trapped rodent running the wheel in its cage. I didn't say anything. My brain wouldn't work.

"I think you should get a lawyer," Mr. Rose said softly.

Julia and I looked at each other with bewilderment. I rarely saw Julia look so confused. The office was silent except for the clicking of Mr. Rose's paper clip on the desk.

"Mr. Rose, where would we find a lawyer in this country? There's not even a Canadian embassy in Laos to advise us," Julia said.

"I don't know," he replied. "I've never been in this situation before. Would someone at your office know?"

"I'm not sure."

I knew she'd be humiliated to ask someone in her office. I sat there, on the periphery, listening to them talk about what to do.

"One of the investigative police officers, Mr. Phon, would like to meet with you to explain what the charges are," Mr. Rose said.

Julia stood to leave. She looked like a lost child. I suddenly understood how my temper had hurt her. I nodded at Mr. Rose and followed her out of the office. As we rode home in a *tuk-tuk* she reached over to clasp my hand and I did not pull it away.

>

There was no indication that the office housed Laos's investigative police. From outside, the dilapidated wooden house looked like any one of the ever-present beer shops that decorated Vientiane's streets. A big yellow Beerlao sign hung out front and underneath it a middle-aged woman sold steaming bowls of noodle soup to hungry passersby.

"Mr. Phon, *yu boh*?" I asked her. She pointed upstairs.

Julia followed me up the rickety wooden steps and I knocked on the hollow door at the top.

"Ah, Mr. Cameron and Mrs. Julia. Do come in. I've heard all about you," Mr. Phon said, his grin exposing a mouth of missing teeth.

We followed the extremely short man into his office. The drab, dirty-yellow colour, the posters peeling off the wall, and the sullied fake flowers gave the office a sad air of someone who once dreamed of big things. On the bureau sat a large framed picture of Mr. Phon in a suit with the same fake grin he had given us. Mr. Rose said that Mr. Phon had studied law abroad, but being a lawyer from a country with few enforced laws meant that he was jobless when he returned to Laos. Even when he did find work as an investigative police officer he wasn't very busy. Mr. Rose explained that the truth usually isn't hard to find because of the smallness of Vientiane's neighbourhoods, and the interconnectedness of the people.

"Where is your lawyer?" Mr. Phon looked around the room for someone he obviously knew wouldn't be there.

"We haven't been able to get in touch with the Canadian embassy in Bangkok yet," Julia said.

Mr. Phon nodded slowly. I felt as vulnerable as a child who'd just wet his pants.

"What are the charges, sir?" Julia asked.

"It's interesting you should ask, Mrs. Julia. The first charge is assault causing bodily harm."

"What do you mean 'the first charge'?" she asked. "There are more?"

"Shortly after Mr. Cameron's name came across my desk for assault, I heard his name mentioned in association with another crime against our people."

"What?" Suddenly I couldn't hear properly.

"Mr. Cameron, did you have a Lao girlfriend?" Mr. Phon's English made the question seem all the more abrupt. It shoved me out of my daze.

"Pardon?" My head reeled. "I don't understand."

"A girlfriend who died."

"What? How do you know about her?"

"Where were you on the night of April 14th, 2000?"

I looked at Julia. Why was he asking me this stuff?

"Cameron, don't answer him, please," Julia said. "Mr. Phon, we need a lawyer."

"Since you asked, Mrs. Julia, the second charge is manslaughter."

The world screeched to a halt. My head flopped forward.

"What are you talking about?" Julia said in a wavering voice. My eyes were closed. I wanted to reach across the desk and squeeze Mr. Phon's neck until his eyes popped out.

Julia buried her head in her hands. I could hear her sniffing back tears.

"Mr. Cam, can you tell me how much you drank at the Lao New Year party?"

"I wasn't at the Lao New Year party."

"So drunk you can't even remember, hey." He snorted a chuckle.

"No, Mr. Phon —"

"We have reports that you were there.

"I was supposed to be there but —"

"Cam, please," Julia said, black rivers of mascara running down her cheeks. "Do not say anything. Not until we get some legal help."

"Mrs. Julia, may I remind you that you are not in Canada anymore," Mr. Phon said. "We do things differently here. Our legal processes don't take nearly as much time as yours."

"From what I hear you have no legal processes," Julia said.

"You people always think your way of doing things is better," Mr Phon replied, annoyed. "Cameron, Mr. Khamdeng, who hosted the party, said that Nok invited you. It was his bike, but he wasn't driving. He has an alibi. The faster we do this, the better. The government is breathing down my back to solve this one. They want to see the foreigner responsible for killing a Lao daughter put in jail."

"Jail?" Julia said forcefully, the *J* popping out of her mouth vehemently. "Jail?"

This could not be happening. It just couldn't. I was petrified.

"Assault. Manslaughter. We can't have this danger to Lao people walking free in Vientiane," said Mr. Phon. "Local people were harmed or killed in both cases. It's my job to protect my fellow citizens and I take my job very seriously." He stared at me. "*Very* seriously."

"But I wasn't at the party. I was in Vang Vieng."

"Can you prove it?"

"Yes, my friend was with me. Somchai. He lives next door."

Mr. Phon looked disappointed. He scratched his head and made some notes.

"Okay, then how about this basketball fight? Did you do it?"

"Mr. Phon, we're leaving. This is ridiculous. My son's not admitting to anything. We need some kind of lawyer here."

"Suit yourself, madam."

Julia stood up and grabbed my hand, squeezing it hard. It felt good to have her clutching on to me like that. I followed her outside and was relieved that it was pouring down rain by the bucketful so no one could see my watery eyes.

Julia was on the phone with the Canadian Department of Foreign Affairs in Ottawa when they came for me. There were three of them in green-beige uniforms, each with a pistol at his side.

"You are being charged with assault causing bodily harm and manslaughter. You will be held until there is a trial," one of the police officers said in broken English.

I just stood there, stunned, while another handcuffed me.

Julia began to scream. "You can't do this! You can't just jail someone without some kind of legal decision." She was pale with terror.

"There was a legal decision," the lead officer said. "To put him in jail."

"But he wasn't there to defend himself. He hasn't done anything wrong." She grabbed at the officer leading me into the back of a rusty black truck.

"Two local people are his victims. A Thai and a Lao." He gently tried to push her off of him, but she kept lunging back. Finally the two other officers held on to her arms as they loaded me into the truck. An icy chill climbed up my back.

"Cam!" She started to scream. "They're taking my son! Help me, someone!" I heard her cry and saw her body heave as the truck's engine started.

"Julia!" I yelled. I struggled to free my arms from the handcuffs. "Let me go!" I screamed at the guards. "I didn't do anything! You can't do this!" Their faces were stony and silent, although I thought I detected a look of pity in one man's eyes.

I watched from the back of the truck as my mother doubled over, clutching her middle, and got smaller and smaller in the distance.

FISHBONE

Seng

Vong and Seng stood near a food vendor's ramshackle stall in the busy Thai Morning Market in Nong Khai. Women with babies tied to their backs pressed past them. Men in tank tops and ripped shorts followed, pushing large carts filled with the women's purchases of cooking oil, dish soap, and rice, forcing Seng to squeeze closer to his sister to make room. Across from them, a woman sold meat. Fatty flanks of beef lay in the morning sun as flies danced around and pools of blood gathered. The woman counted out change to a customer on a dead pig's body.

Vong ate spicy papaya salad and sticky rice with her fingers. She ate voraciously, but Seng couldn't. He knew he was hungry, but his nerves wouldn't let him eat. The weight of what they had just done sat heavily on his shoulders. He had fled the scene of an accident, evaded the Lao authorities, and entered Thailand illegally. To think that last week he had been a poor, nameless peddler of cheap Chinese goods. But then again, last week he'd had a little sister.

"Papaya salad doesn't taste the same here," Vong said, interrupting his painful thoughts. "No *padek*."

Seng didn't know how she was able to think about fermented fish sauce at a time like this. He could barely think. Everything that had just happened was jumbled up in his head.

"I have to eat before I can think," Vong said, apparently reading his thoughts. When she was finally finished she licked her fingers and whispered, "I think we should travel deeper into Thailand. Get away from the border." She looked around to make sure no one could hear her. The northeastern Thais could understand Lao well. "Let's take the train into Bangkok, like we planned. But we'll have to watch our money, I don't have much."

Seng nodded, but he didn't understand how she could live in Canada and not have much money. Maybe Canadians didn't have as much money as Amercians.

They climbed onto the overnight train to Bangkok for the long journey. When they first boarded they sat in silence on the hard, wooden third-class seats. Seng was worried about drawing attention to themselves. The clickety-clack sound of the train floated in through the open windows and filled the silence between them. At first peddlers, too young to be by themselves on a train bound for Bangkok, strode up and down the aisles, selling bread, commercial cakes wrapped in clear plastic, toothbrushes and toothpaste. Seng didn't look up at them. He didn't want to make eye contact with anyone. As they chugged farther away from Nong Khai the little vendors got off at a stop and disappeared into the twilight. The journey grew longer and the seats seemed harder; he was thankful when Vong took out a thin, plastic photo album she had brought with her. Something to distract him.

"In case I miss home," she explained. *Wasn't Lao her home?* He tried not to let his disappointment show when she pointed to a picture of her husband, Chit, with their house in the background. He had always imagined she lived in a house like he saw on TV: giant and brick in a neighbourhood surrounded by similar giant, brick houses. An oversized box store down the road. A "subdivision," they called it. But from the pictures Seng could see that his sister's tiny house was made of aluminum siding and had faded, flaking paint on the shutters. She explained that it was not a full house, but half a house, with another family living in the other half. A "duplex," she called it. She showed him pictures of her and Chit inside, standing along a flimsy stair rail, or sitting on brown, thin carpet. Where were the houses he had seen in the movies? The huge, airy houses with double-car garages and swimming pools in the backyards?

"Canada has those," Vong explained when he asked. "I just can't afford to live in one."

"But you work."

"I'm a cashier at a grocery store. Chit works for a toy company. We work, but life is expensive. I told you, we're going to have to watch our expenses in Bangkok."

"Do you own a car?"

"I take the bus."

Seng was glad when the conductor came by to check their tickets. He didn't want her to see his disappointment. Vong started to talk about when she had first arrived in

Canada. He guessed it was to keep her mind busy. She laughed as she talked about her first time in a Canadian bathroom. She couldn't find the bidet anywhere.

"You mean they dry wipe?" Seng asked, disgusted. His friends had told him stories about how Westerners didn't use water after a crap, but he always thought they were just saying it for effect.

She talked about how no one thought she was a foreigner in Canada because most people come from somewhere else, how the winter could be so cold that your eyelashes feel like they're freezing shut and how Canadians only eat certain parts of chickens, like the breasts or wings.

"What about the feet?" Seng asked.

"Can't even get them at the grocery store."

"What about from your neighbours?"

"My neighbours don't raise chickens." Vong laughed.

Of course they don't, Seng thought and reddened. He didn't know a thing about the world.

"But what do they do with them? The feet, I mean. Canadian chickens must have feet."

She laughed and shrugged.

"*Euaigh*, why did you never answer me?"

"The e-mails, you mean?"

Of course that is what I mean. He nodded.

"I didn't know what to say …"

"But didn't you miss us? Didn't you want to know about us?"

"I read every word of your e-mails, Seng. I knew how you were doing."

"But you didn't reply?"

"And tell you that I don't live in your beloved America? Or that I don't have enough money to bring you to live with me? Then you would know how I've failed."

"How you've failed? What are you talking about?"

He looked out the window to see the sun painting the sky pink, like the colour of skin around the perimeter of a wound. It dipped into the horizon, finally deserting the day for good. He didn't want it to get dark. He wanted Vong to go back to talking about bathrooms and chicken feet and everyday things. Maybe it would fill up the space in his head so there would be no room for the hurt lodged in his throat like a fishbone.

He remembered the concern in Nok's eyes as he'd gotten on the motorbike, the secure feeling of having her capable body behind him. The look of that same body flung across the road, leg at an unnatural angle, eyes wide open. Seng had turned away from the sight, but he could not turn away from his mind. He began to rock back and forth in his seat. The sun vanished completely and the darkness swallowed him up. Vong, quiet now, reached out and gently placed her hand on his knee.

CAPTURED

Cam

The red dirt driveway of Khang Khok Prison was inappropriately cheery. It snaked through a grey, concrete wall with a barbed-wire fence on top. A tower loomed high, overlooking two cellblocks, one for women and the other for men. From outside the buildings didn't look much different from others in Vientiane. They had sun-baked, rusty, red roofs and porches stretching the entire length of the one-storey buildings. White paint flaked off their wooden siding. But inside was different.

The wooden leg blocks were the first thing I noticed when they brought me into the cellblock — my hands cuffed together and the sweaty, brown palm of a prison guard pushing into my back. My heartbeat thrummed in my ears and I wondered if I was really processing everything. Wooden blocks? Through the steel bars of a cell door I looked to see them clamped onto a black man's feet so he couldn't walk. He lay on his back in a pool of his own piss. I could see where his pants were wet around his crotch. Five other men — his cellmates — crowded around him in the small cell. I swallowed. My injured ankle gave out and I stumbled. The guard yanked me up, but then he breathed something into my ear — I couldn't understand what, but his tone sounded surprisingly kind. He pressed his hand into my back and guided me to my cell.

An outhouse stench hung so heavily in the air I could taste it. Through a tiny open window I could hear chickens clucking and palm trees rustling, as if life were perfectly normal. Then I was shown to my cell, and met the eyes of the four inmates I would share the small space with. I hoped they couldn't see how much I was trembling. I had never been so scared in my life.

Only foreigners went to Khang Khok — apparently the jails for Lao people were worse. From what I could tell, a lot of the prisoners looked Thai or Vietnamese. Some were African. In my cell was Tong, a Thai arrested for drug trafficking; Danh, a Vietnamese guy caught with heroin; and Huang, an old Chinese man with one gummy eye sealed shut. I couldn't piece together what he was in prison for. The only one who spoke English was a thin, bald Thai guy named Sai, whose English was good and reminded me of Somchai's way of speaking. I nervously scanned the small cell for my bunk.

"We sleep on the floor," Sai said. "One blanket between the five of us. Doesn't matter much during the dry season, but when it's cool you have to make a deal with Huang. He controls the blanket."

My hands shook as I changed out of my clothes into the torn prison uniform a guard had shoved into my hands. I think it was supposed to be white, but was now a drab grey. I could barely manage the buttons. From the corner of my eye I saw a prisoner on his knees in the damp hallway outside our cell. A guard hovered over top of him, barking something in Lao.

"You can never be higher than some of the guards," Sai explained. "Have to stay on your knees when you talk to them. Others are a bit gentler. What are you here for, anyway?"

"Nothing." I slumped on the wooden floor in a corner, my back against the concrete wall.

Sai laughed. "That's what we all say. What are the charges?"

"Assault causing bodily harm. Had a fight during a basketball game." I didn't tell Sai about the manslaughter charges.

"Must have been a bad fight."

"That's what they say. I'm just here until they complete the investigation."

Sai smiled sadly. "I've been waiting three years for a trial."

"Three years! They can't do that."

"They can do whatever they want. The communists burned the national constitution back in the seventies. There are no laws, or at least none that are enforced in any kind of consistent way."

"The Canadian government will get me out."

"Yes. You're allowed one-fifteen minute visit from them a month, if the police allow. There were a couple of Kiwis in here. Their government got them out, although it took five years."

I felt sick. I went around the corner into the tiny bathroom. There was no door. The toilet was a hole in the ground with foot-grips on either side. Beside it was a thin, concrete trough filled with water. A small, red plastic bucket sat on its slimy edge. My whole body was shaking.

Why was I here? Where was the driver of the bike that Nok had fallen from? I didn't think her brother could drive a motorbike. Could it have been the drunk French guy? I splashed water from the bucket over my face and then poured it over my head. The cool water trickled down my back. I wanted to wash all of this away. It couldn't be real. Any minute some Canadian official in a suit would walk up to the cell, call out my name, and unlock the door.

When I came out of the bathroom Huang was slumped in a corner with his head hung between his knees. I could hear him snoring. Danh and Tong were gone. Sai was sitting cross-legged in the middle of the cell, his hands resting on his knees, his back ramrod-straight and his eyes closed. He breathed deeply. Was he meditating or was he a mental case? I could hear the air rushing in and out through his nostrils. One inhale seemed to take forever. With each exhale his belly sunk into his spine and his ribs stuck out. I could count each rib if I wanted to.

Turns out there wasn't anything else to do in the cell but count Sai's ribs. No books or magazines were allowed. I lay on the wooden floorboards and tried to close my eyes, but that would just make the thoughts race faster through my head. I thought about Julia and her bitter screams. What had my temper done to her?

The clanging of the steel bar door as its sliding bolts unlocked interrupted my thoughts. Sai's eyes opened.

"Dinner time," he said.

A toothless prison guard slid one bowl of watery soup along the floor and a basket of sticky rice.

"Who's it for?" I asked, wondering what was floating in the soup.

"It's for us all. One bowl per room," Sai said. He had to be joking.

He rolled a ball of sticky rice in his right hand and passed it to me. I wasn't hungry, but I thought food might stop my shakes. I gingerly bit into the ball of rice. Sai ate hungrily, slurping as he spooned the soup into his mouth. Huang raised his head to see what was going on, and then hung it again with disinterest. Suddenly something hard cracked between my molars. I raised a hand to my cheek and tried to pry the small pebble out with my tongue. I watched Sai as he used his fingers to pick his teeth. Then I watched him wipe his mouth with the back of his hand, push the bowl aside. There was nothing else to do but watch him. He stood up, placed his hands on his lower back and leaned back to stretch. He walked to the bathroom. I felt anxiety creep up in my throat. My legs started to get jumpy. I drummed my fingers on the floor.

"They'll take you to work tomorrow," he said when he came out.

As the cell grew darker, a guard wearing a green uniform brought Danh and Tong back. They undressed and lay on the floor in their underwear. They looked exhausted. Before long I knew they were sleeping by the deepening of their breath. I sat and watched as the cell grew black. It was like I was watching a movie. It wasn't real. Finally the cell was completely dark. There was nothing left to watch. I closed my eyes, but my rushing thoughts kept sleep far away.

MESS

Seng

Seng was comforted by the crowd they had to jostle through to find a cheap Bangkok guesthouse. The sidewalks were heaving with people: well-dressed teenagers laughing into their cellphones; dirty, poor children with their wild brown hair and palms held up to sunburned tourists; businesspeople in suits and skirts. There was no way he and Vong would be spotted in the middle of them all.

Seng wasn't sure how to work the shower in their small room. At home he always used a bucket to pour water over himself. He didn't want to ask Vong how to use it. He could take care of himself. He eyed the gleaming silver handle and pulled it up. Water flowed out of the tap. Easy enough, but how could he get it to come out of the showerhead? He fiddled around with the handle, making the water hot and cold. Then he noticed the little metal rod on top of the tap. He pulled it up and the water shot through the showerhead, piercing his body. *See?* he thought, *I can figure things out for myself.*

After his shower, he fell onto the thin bed of the guest-room, exhausted. A ceiling fan whirred overhead.

"So when do we go to Canada?" he asked.

Vong looked up from the crumpled map she was reading, surprised.

"Seng, you don't have a passport. How can we go to Canada?" She looked annoyed by his question.

"I thought that was the plan, *euaigh*. Bangkok and then Canada."

"I said Bangkok and then we'll see."

That was not how he remembered it. He had to stop relying on her so much. He needed to come up with his own plan. Why was she here, anyway? She should go back to her easy life with Chit. It was what she had left them for, after all.

Vong looked guilty. "Don't worry about it, little brother. What we need right now is sleep. We'll decide tomorrow."

He gave her a weak smile and turned over on his side to sleep. She climbed onto the bed beside him — they could only afford a room with one bed.

"You sleep the same way you did as a kid. With your legs curled and your hand tucked in between your knees," she said. "Do you remember how we used to sleep side by side on the floor of the Luang Prabang house? On full-moon nights we could see the mango tree from the window. Remember making bets about who would be able to reach the highest mango the next day?"

"You always got it, Vong. The mango."

Vong laughed.

"Tell me something about our mother," he said. Maybe it would make him feel better.

She shifted in the bed.

"Like what?"

"I don't know. A good memory of her."

"Well, let's see. When I was young I dreamed of being a dancer in the king's court. Did you know that?"

"No."

He didn't want to know about her, he wanted to know about their mother.

"I was good. One of Meh's friends gave me lessons. The king's dancers used to talk about me, how I would dance for him one day." She rolled over to look at Seng. "One time Meh snuck me in to watch the Laos National Ballet. I remember giggling and hiding with her behind a thick, musty-smelling curtain as we watched the dancers. It was the Ramayana story. I can still see the silky wave of long hair down the back of the dancer who played Sita." She paused, as if she was savouring the memory.

"You know what I remember most of all?" she asked.

He didn't answer.

"I remember the looks on the dancers' faces. The glimmer of someone practising something they truly love. You know that look? Now I'm just a cashier at a grocery store."

That's better than peddling cheap plastic goods, he thought. He was getting tired of her. Did she think of anyone but herself? He rolled over and tried deepening his breath so she'd think he was asleep, even though he hadn't truly slept since Nok had died.

Since Nok was *killed*.

"Nothing but a cashier, and I can't even have a baby," she said into the night. "That's what the doctors say. Something's wrong with me. I can't get pregnant."

His heart softened.

"So sorry to hear that, sister," he said.

"I really want to be a mother. To know what's it like to love someone like that."

He wondered what it would be like to be loved so unconditionally. His sisters loved him, he knew that. And Khamdeng. But he didn't think anything could compare to the feel of a mother's love.

From the hall outside of their room he heard backpackers, their voices thick with drink and excitement, returning to the guesthouse for the night. He heard the slap of the staff's flip-flops as they showed late-arriving guests to their rooms. Gradually the noise waned and the guesthouse was shrouded in the silent blackness of very late at night.

"We should sleep," she said.

"Yes," he said, rolling over and feeling very alone, even though the bed they were sharing was crowded with their two round bodies.

EVERY SINGLE DAY

Cam

I didn't know where the guard was taking me. He called me toward the cell door with a rough hand gesture, handcuffed me, and led me down a corridor slick with some kind of fluid. My heart pounded violently. He led me outside, past murky brown ponds. I could barely open my eyes in the sun's intensity. We passed the interrogation room, where I heard the screams of a grown man and the smell of something burning. I tried to swallow, but couldn't. My legs felt like jelly, but I knew things would be worse if I stopped walking. Finally, he pushed me toward the visitor's hut, where Julia and Meh Mee were waiting.

It felt like a month had passed since I'd seen Julia, but she said it had been six days. She gasped when she saw me, brought a hand to her mouth. Then she hugged me so tightly I lost my breath. I shook in her arms. She would make it okay. She would carry me away from here. When we pulled away, her shoulder was soaked with my tears.

"I came every day and they wouldn't let me in." Dark blue circles cupped her wet eyes. "Finally, I brought Meh

Mee. She talked to the guards in Lao and they agreed to a bribe." Meh Mee smiled sadly at me.

A guard watched us from the corner of the damp room. A pistol hung from his hip. Dust motes floated in the sunlight streaming in through the dark-brown slats of the wooden hut. Julia smelled like the outside — alive and clean. She reached into her stuffed canvas bag and passed me crackers, a big bottle of juice, and a jar of peanut butter. She ripped the tinfoil off a small pizza from a French restaurant. The steam streamed up towards the mouldy rafters. My hands were so shaky she had to hold it up to my mouth to eat. It felt warm and substantial in my mouth. I closed my eyes and noticed the tang of the sauce, the thickness of the cheese, and the crispness of the green pepper. I had never tasted pizza so delicious.

"The Canadian government is on our case, Cam." I liked how she said *our*, as if I wasn't alone. "They're sending a rep from the Australian embassy until a Canadian official can get here. The Australian should be meeting with you any day now."

"When?"

"We don't know. But soon."

I looked down in my lap.

"I'm trying, honey. I am doing everything I can." She started to cry. I looked at Meh Mee.

"Where's Somchai?"

Julia wiped her nose and reached for my hands. The room was silent.

"Where's Somchai?" I asked again.

"The investigative police interviewed him." Julia looked away.

"What do you mean?"

"They wanted him to say he wasn't in Vang Vieng with you on the night that Nok was killed. He wouldn't do it."

Meh Mee looked down in her lap, fingered her worn *sin*.

"He was beaten up badly, Cam. But he's going to be okay."

I pushed away the pizza she was holding up to my mouth. I bit my lower lip. Silence was all around. This was too much. Anger welled up inside of me, but this time I didn't need to count it away. Fear was doing it for me. I had heard the shrieks of prisoners being punished for bad behaviour. I was so powerless.

"He's going to be okay, Cam," Julia squeezed my hand tightly. Meh Mee nodded at me. I couldn't speak.

The guard walked towards us, pulled Meh Mee up roughly by her arm.

"We have to go now. They would only give us fifteen minutes. I will come every day, Cam. Every single day." Julia's voice cracked. Tears streamed down her cheeks. What was I doing to them all? Everyone I cared about was suffering and it was all my fault.

She turned around to take one last look. I held up a trembling hand to wave to her.

"Every single day, Cam. I will be at those prison gates."

"Thanks, Mom," I said. It was the first time I had called her "Mom" in eleven years. The word felt good in my mouth, round, soft, and reassuring.

BREATHE

Cam

Sai and I sat in the cell, staring at each other without even noticing it. Or at least I didn't notice it. Sai seemed to notice everything. I was so bored out of my mind I stared at him all the time. He fascinated me. The way nothing seemed to bother him, not even when the guards spoke to him like he was a dog. The way his breath got deep and loud when there was a commotion in the prison — a man screaming out as his legs were clamped with wooden blocks, or cellmates arguing loudly with each other in the middle of the night. It was like he would almost relax into the disturbing moment, instead of wishing it away. Sometimes he would close his eyes for hours on end with his back as straight as the bars on our cell. When he was like that his belly would move in and out with his breath while the corners of his mouth turned up in a slight smile. I was sharing a cell with the Buddha himself.

One night I was led back to the cell after a day of weeding the prison vegetable garden in torrential rain. It was August, the wettest month of the Lao year. I was covered in a thick layer of slick red mud. The prison guard hadn't even let me stop to go to the bathroom. I had to piss right there in between the wormy tomatoes and cilantro. As I pulled thorny weeds all I could think about was Somchai. What had the police done to him? By the time the grey day began to fade into black I was so mad that I was getting freaked out. I was afraid that I would explode and be taken to the interrogation room, and afraid of the rumours I heard of men being burned or whipped.

After the guard locked our cell door and was out of earshot, I peeled my soaking uniform away from my now-scrawny body and chucked each piece across the cell so they slapped against the prison wall and splattered mud everywhere. I grabbed the bucket for our makeshift shower and chucked it against the wall so hard it cracked. Huang looked up from his snoring. His lifeless eyes told me he had seen outbursts like this so many times he couldn't care less. I began to pound the hard cement wall with my fists.

"Breathe, my friend," Sai said.

"Fuck off, Sai. People have been telling me that my whole life."

"Yeah, but do you know *how* to breathe?" he asked in a way that didn't make me feel like an idiot.

He walked over and gently took hold of my wrist. He stared at me with brown eyes that were soft and steady at the same time. I felt something inside me shift, although my heart still flailed violently in my ribcage. My shoulders dropped away from my ears. The knots of tension in my back muscles softened. He led me to sit beside him on the hard prison floor.

"Belly relaxes out on the inhale, comes in towards the spine on the exhale. Close your mouth and do it through your nose. It filters the air."

He closed his eyes and placed his hands in prayer at his heart. His breath sounded like waves. I closed my eyes and copied its slow rhythm. It was bizarre, but why not? There was nothing else to do.

"Now try breathing one breath per minute. You'll never feel depressed." He flickered his eyes open briefly to speak.

"One breath a minute? How is that possible?"

"Inhale through your nose for twenty seconds, hold your breath for twenty seconds and exhale out your nose for twenty seconds. I'll count for you."

"I feel like I'm going to pass out," I said after trying it.

"Okay, start with eight seconds and work your way up day by day."

"This is weird."

"Just do it and then tell me what's weird."

We stayed like that for a long time, sitting beside one another, inhaling and exhaling. When we finished, I collapsed onto my place on the hard floor and slept a deep, dreamless sleep.

➤

"Why are you here, anyway?" I asked him the next morning.

"Karma," he replied. "Learning from the mistakes of my past."

Then he told me his story in a steady rhythm. He was a Buddhist monk who had once lived in a monastery on a remote Thai island. He said there were more birds, lizards, and frogs on that island then there were people. It was surrounded by the sapphire Gulf of Thailand and brimming with lush, green jungle. One day a Hmong-American tourist was sailing around the southern tip of Thailand and stopped at the island. He visited the temple at the small monastery every day and he and Sai became good friends. He told Sai about his people, the Hmong, an ethnic minority in Southeast Asia. Droves of them fled from Laos to Thailand in the 1970s because they were facing violence and persecution for fighting against the communists. Nearly thirty years later, they were being forced back. Some Hmong who returned to Laos were never seen again. Others were thrust into political re-education camps. Most faced discrimination.

After his friend left, Sai's conscience told him he needed to do something. He wrote letters to the Thai government demanding that Hmong people wanting to remain in Thailand be allowed to do so. He travelled to Wat Tham Krabok, a Buddhist monastery in the middle of Thailand where ten thousand Hmong were seeking refuge. There he heard more stories of persecution. He decided to travel across the Mekong into Laos to see what peace he could bring. He was in Vietiane for less than a week when he was imprisoned for political crimes.

"And you've never had a trial?" I asked.

"No."

I heard the sliding locks slip out of their receptacle. It was time to work. I hoped I would be assigned to the same task as Sai, but I wasn't. I never was. I chopped wood for the rest of the day and was glad for my long, deep breaths, slowly taking me far away from my prisons.

SPRING ROLL LADY

Seng

Seng wandered through Bangkok streets, keeping his head down to avoid making eye contact with anyone. He didn't know where he was going, but he didn't care. He was out on his own, walking down the street by himself, finding his own path, not following anyone. He could do this.

He kept walking until he began to feel tired. He looked up briefly to read a street sign. He was on Khaosan Road. It was packed with businesses advertising to tourists. AUTHENTIC THAI MASSAGE HERE! screamed one sign. CHEAP INTERNET ACCES said another. Thai women stood in front of the stores, passing out flyers and convincing backpackers to come inside. Sweaty and tanned Europeans, North Americans, and Australians milled around street vendors selling slushy lemonade or T-shirts with Thai lettering. Seng watched them, fascinated. He had never seen so many foreigners in one place before. Is this what it would feel like to be in America? The thought made him sad. He would never go to America now. He found the stoop of a closed-up shop and sat there, watching from the sidelines.

As the hot sun rose in the sky his stomach began to rumble. He couldn't remember the last time he'd eaten. Amidst the bustle, he spotted an older woman selling greasy, fried spring rolls. He fingered the Thai coins in his pocket. A tourist had given them to him for a squirt gun for Lao New Year. He had packed the *baht* when he was fleeing home. He would buy himself something to eat. He didn't need to rely on Vong.

Seng watched the spring roll woman carefully as she counted out his change. Something had given him pause. Despite the scarf around her head, the farmer's hat and the dark sunglasses, something about her seemed familiar. He couldn't say why. She didn't look at him as she counted out his spring rolls and handed him his *baht* with a wrinkly, thin hand.

He took his change and thanked her.

"*Kop jai,*" he said without thinking.

The woman looked at him abruptly, a puzzled look on her face.

Damn, he thought. He had spoken in Lao. Vong would have never made such a careless mistake.

The woman stared with her mouth hanging open, as if he were a ghost that had just appeared. He was suddenly terrified. Did she know who he was? Was there a search warrant out for his arrest? He turned on his heel and walked quickly away. He needed to find the guesthouse.

He walked in the direction he'd come from, but couldn't remember whether to turn left or right off Khaosan Road. He looked over his shoulder to see if the woman was watching him, but she was gone, merged into the crowd. The streets teemed with people. Bangkok was such a loud, swarming city compared to Vientiane. He was disoriented. He began to walk east. He walked until he was so thirsty he had to stop and look for water. The sun was starting to dip in the sky. He really hoped he was going in the right direction, but as the sky grew darker his doubts grew bigger. *I should have brought a map*, he thought. He wished Vong was there. When the sky was finally completely black he hailed a *tuk-tuk* and told the driver the name of the guesthouse. He paid the driver all of the *baht* he had left. As they wobbled back to the guesthouse Seng tried to remember every detail of the streets, the soy-milk vendor on this corner, the big French supermarket on another.

When he finally let himself into their guesthouse room, Vong was in a panic.

"Where were you?" she asked breathlessly.

"Out," he said, and liked the confused look on her face. *I don't need you to watch over me*, he thought. *I can do things on my own. I'm not as stupid as you think.*

That night as he and Vong lay sleepless in bed he thought about the Canadian boy. He wondered if the police had found him. Guilt pressed down on him, dark and hard, so that he felt like he couldn't breathe. He tried to brush the thoughts out of his mind. He thought of the spring-roll woman instead.

"How tall was Meh?" he asked Vong.

"Shorter than us," she said. "Maybe a metre sixty or so? Why?"

"Just wondering," he said.

JAILBREAK

Cam

Sai and I made a deal with the guards. We gave them the little bit of money that Julia would slip into my hand during her visit. The money was to buy food for the catfish that swam in the murky trenches and ponds on the prison grounds. In exchange we were given fish to eat and wood to build a cooking fire. The protein helped to bolster my energy, and soon my ribs weren't sticking out quite as far.

August, the wettest month of the year, set a permanent, depressing grey cloud over Khang Khok Prison. The sound of downpours on the prison roof became monotonous. Work on the prison grounds was like a giant mud-wrestling match. I remembered what Nok had said about the Mekong swelling at this time of year. I wondered if downtown Vientiane was flooding. I'd been in Laos for eight months. I should have hated this country even more than when I'd first arrived. But there was something about it that had snaked its way into my heart. Something gentle, accepting, and strangely freeing, despite the harsh government rules. I liked how slowly people moved. How in the end all they really wanted was to laugh and make jokes with their friends and family. For a small, land-locked country there seemed to be so much space. So much room in a friendship, so much time in a minute. Or maybe all of the breathing I was doing with Sai was making me loopy.

Summer slipped into a cool, damp Lao autumn. I still hadn't had a trial. For one gruelling week in November we were not permitted to leave the cell, not even for work. We didn't see the light of day. Sai said most of the guards were off for the That Luang festival. The jail was operating with a skeleton staff. One day there wasn't even a guard to bring us our rice and measly bowl of broth.

I remembered how Nok had said she would take me to the festival. It had seemed so far away from that night in April. I would never have imagined that when it came she would be dead and I would be in prison.

The nights had turned so cold that I would wake up to find myself shivering and huddled into Sai's back on the floor. Back home I would have been creeped out about sleeping closely to so many guys, but you don't think about that kind of stuff when you're just trying to survive. Besides, Lao guys never think about it. They walk down the street with one arm draped around their guy friend and no one thinks twice. In Canada we're so free, but at the same time we're not.

Shivering through the night, the one big blanket we had to share between the five cellmates became a problem. Huang was the master of it. Throughout the night he'd be cocooned in the faded fleece blanket while the rest of us shivered and our teeth chattered. I guessed he had seniority because he'd been in here for so long. Either that or no one wanted to piss him off for some reason I didn't understand.

"What do we do to get some blanket?" I asked Sai after one almost sleepless night. I pointed at Danh still sleeping beside Huang, his body ramrod straight and the both of them covered with the grey, holey thing.

"Forget about it. Better to learn how to sleep in any situation."

That morning, one of the few guards remaining made me spend the day cleaning up catfish caught from the prison's trenches. Most of them would be sold at the nearby market. The guards would pocket the cash. I slipped some *kip* that Julia had given me during our last visit into the guard's hand so at least one of the fish would be for Sai and me. At first the smell and sight of so many fish guts made me want to puke. I didn't know where to begin. I'd never cleaned a fish before.

"You don't know how?" the guard asked, slapping me lightly on the back of my head. "Every idiot knows how to clean a fish. Your father not teach you anything?"

He showed me how to take each clammy, slippery fish in my hand and slice its jelly-like underside open with a knife. He stuck a thick, grimy finger into the fish's belly and dug around until he pulled out a clear, transparent organ, long and slimy.

"There, now do them all," he said, after the fish in his hand had been totally gutted. He pointed to a heap of limp, black catfish surrounded by a crowd of happy flies.

By the time I was finished I was covered in fish guts and slime. I reeked like death. If I hadn't been so starving I don't think I would have ever eaten fish again.

The guard ordered me to light a fire and gave me the biggest fish in the pile to cook for Sai and me. I had noticed that every now and then a guard would let his harsh exterior slip, let the Lao in him shine through. Sai said they were just fathers trying to feed their families, after all. My stomach growled. We'd only had sticky rice and watery pork-fat soup all week.

The guard led me back to the cell; his keys jangled against the cold hard bars as he slid open the locks and opened the door. Huang was sitting in the corner, head hung between this knees like always. But this time his head snapped up as the guard slid the locks shut behind us.

"You have fish?" he asked. It was the first time I had heard him speak English.

"Yeah."

"You give to Huang."

So far there hadn't been any problems in the cell with us eating fish. I figured they all worked their own deals so they could have some, too.

"No way," I said.

"Okay, you give me Sai's share." Huang's gummy eye was sealed shut, his dark lashes stuck together with some disgusting goop.

"Not on your life." There was no way I was going to betray Sai. He was keeping me alive in this nightmare.

"You think Sai so good. Sai no better than me. You stay cold. When you tired of freezing you come see Huang, if Sai doesn't get you first." His good eye winked at me as I got ready to take a shower. I decided to place the fish in a bucket just outside the shower so Huang couldn't get his hands on it.

The water felt good as it slid down my sweaty back, but

the few minutes I had to myself created too much space for thoughts. Could anyone in this country really prove that I didn't kill Nok? I let out a long exhale. It didn't work. The lack of sleep combined with malnutrition was making my mind do funny things. I thought about what might happen if I smashed through the small slit of a window in the bathroom. I knew I had to help myself somehow. I couldn't just sit around waiting for other people to decide if I was going to be freed or not. I poured the water over my head faster and faster, hoping it would wash away the fear. Finally I heard Sai's voice as the guard let him into the cell after his day of work. I dried off with a thin, scratchy towel and rounded the cement corner that separated the small shower area from the cell.

"Good to see you," I said.

"Hey!" Huang lifted his heavy head again. His good eye looked at me, then Sai, then back to me again. "You remember what Huang say."

"Yeah, okay." But I had already forgotten. Something to make me doubt Sai. I would never — I had learned too much about friendship in this country. I thought of Somchai's latest letter.

"Cam! From Somchai!" Sai had exclaimed, picking it up from the place where a guard had slid it underneath our cell door. He was just as excited about it as I was. Contact with the outside world. I had told Sai all about my friend Somchai.

I ripped it open and it felt like I was holding a bag of gold even though the letter was short and written on thin, blue airmail paper. Somchai liked his job at the sandwich shop, his sister was coming to visit from Thailand and

Meh Mee was as gossipy as ever. But my mom, he said, had gotten really quiet. She stayed home all the time, except when she was working; no one came to visit her but Meh Mee and Somchai. *She's not the same, Cam*, he wrote. I chewed on my nails.

That night I couldn't sleep. I was freezing. I could feel goosebumps pricking my skin. In the moonlight I could see Danh lying beside Huang. His face kind of looked like he was in pain or something. I heard Huang's breathy sounds and thought I could see something moving under the blankets. I rolled over to my other side. I hugged my knees, trying to get some warmth. Hours seemed to pass and finally Huang's noisy breathing faded into a soft snore. I remembered his words about Sai. I had to get out of this place. I listened to the footfall of the guard patrolling the verandah outside of the cell. I had heard that they sometimes fell asleep in the middle of the night when they thought their supervisor wouldn't see. They said a Nigerian man had escaped once when the guard patrolling his room had dozed off. No one has heard from him since.

I imagined how it might be to run down that red dusty road and through the prison gates into freedom. How it would be to have some control over my life again. What it would be like now that things were so good between my mom and me. All of a sudden a hand at the small of my back interrupted my thoughts. Gentle and soft, like a bird fluttering by.

Sai.

I shifted farther away from him. He seemed to roll in towards me. I could feel his nose pressed into my back. His hand reached for the small of my back again.

"What the fuck?" I brushed it violently away.

He sat up and rubbed his eyes, as if I had woken him. Despite the darkness I could see a look of surprise on his face.

"What is it?"

"Don't play stupid. You think I'm like Danh over there? Giving it up for a piece of blanket?"

"Cam — I ..."

"Don't fucking touch me again."

I saw him wince and realized my mistake. He turned his back toward me and I could tell he was working hard to keep his breath long and deep.

Shit. He was the only person who gave a rat's ass about me in this place. I wouldn't give away his piece of fish, but it didn't take me long to betray him with my quick anger. I thought I had learned a lot about friendship in this country, but obviously I was still an idiot. Jail was destroying me. I would find a way to get out.

KHAOSAN ROAD

Seng

This time Seng remembered how to get to Khaosan Road. He walked up and down the bustling tourist area scanning the sidewalks for the spring-roll woman. Hours passed and he couldn't find her. Finally he stopped to ask a street vendor selling pad Thai if he knew her. He didn't want to draw attention to himself, to have another person acknowledge his existence in this city, but he had to know.

"Do you know how many old ladies sell spring rolls around here?" the vendor laughed as he passed hot sauce to a black guy with a Canadian flag sewn on his backpack. Suddenly Seng didn't feel so good. He walked back to the guesthouse, but he came back the next day. He told Vong the walks were doing him good. Helping him to clear his mind.

"Don't you think you should stick around here? Hide out in the room?"

"It's making me crazy, staying in there all the time. Besides, don't you think the guesthouse staff wonder why we never go out?"

"Okay," she said, like she was giving him permission. "Just keep your head down."

The pad Thai vendor laughed when he recognized Seng in the throng.

"You still looking for your lady?" he asked.

Maybe Vong had been right. He should really stay in the room and not risk being noticed. But he had to know.

Suddenly he spotted her. She was wearing the same conical hat and passing a flimsy paper plate with spring rolls to a blonde tourist. He barely even noticed the girl's pretty face. Instead he sat and watched the old woman. He could see her forehead shining with sweat underneath her hat. Her well-worn skirt was decorated with grease stains. Sometimes she would take a break and sit on the curb, rocking back and forth and rubbing her hands up and down her thighs. Something wasn't right with her, but Seng didn't know what. She placed a hand on the small of her back and stood up stiffly, surveying the cement sidewalks for her next point of sale. He strained to hear her through the crowd, but she rarely spoke. He grew more agitated. He needed to know.

She bent over her giant pot of spring rolls as he approached her.

"How many?" she asked, without looking up. Somehow he wasn't surprised to hear her Lao accent. He really should go. If she was Lao, she might have heard about him. But his feet were frozen in place.

"I'm not here for spring rolls." He didn't know what to say now that he had approached her. The woman looked up and then gasped.

"Where are you from?" he asked.

He couldn't see her eyes behind her dark sunglasses, but her head turned slightly from side to side, as if she was scanning the streets anxiously. She acted as if she hadn't heard him.

"Are you Lao?" he asked. She hobbled hurriedly in the direction of the bus stop.

"Wait!" Seng called, but she kept walking. He followed her. She glanced over her shoulder at him and tried to quicken her pace, but Seng caught up to her feeble gait.

"Are you from Luang Prabang?" he called out to the back of her wrinkled brown blouse.

She wheeled around to look at him. She dropped her basket of spring rolls. One rolled out of the basket and onto the grey street littered with cigarette butts. Her jaw briefly dropped.

"Who are you? You are with the Lao government?" She made an effort to stand taller.

"No."

"What do you want?"

"Are you a mother? Of three children?" He couldn't believe he was asking her this. All of the stress must really be weighing on him. But his heart leapt up into his throat. He badly wanted her to say yes.

The woman stood silently for a long time. She looked down at the road and fiddled with the fold of her soiled skirt. She suddenly looked like she had forgotten where she was.

"I must go," she finally said and bent to pick up her basket.

"Don't!"

But she was already shuffling back toward the bus stop.

SUN OF FREEDOM

Cam

The short prison guard missing one yellowed front tooth came for me again. This time I didn't feel like I was going to piss my pants with fear. For some reason the guards didn't bother Sai and me too much. So far I had been spared the wooden leg blocks.

"It's the breath," Sai explained.

"What are you talking about now?" He was always coming up with weird explanations.

"When your breath is deep and strong you are deep and strong. People can sense that. They feel it in your presence. You get a lot more respect."

"If you say so."

Whatever it was, the guard tossed me one tiny slice of kindness that damp afternoon. He told me where he was taking me. I wouldn't have to agonize over whether I was headed for the interrogation room. I wondered if they'd built the visitor's hut right beside the terrifying room on purpose. So they could play cruel mind games with the prisoners.

"Meeting with Australian guy," the guard said, his pink tongue flicking at the doorway of his missing tooth.

My fifteen-minute consular visit. My stomach flipped. Someone besides my mom, Somchai, and Meh Mee actually cared. I mattered.

"I'm Ned Jones," the pale Australian official said, nodding as the guard led me into the clammy visitor hut. With one hairy arm he passed me a plastic shopping bag filled with granola bars, nuts, and beef jerky. I felt like he was handing me a bag of jewels.

"Tough spot, isn't it?"

I nodded, even though the casual way he had said it told me that he had no clue how bad it was. Even still, I felt like hugging the guy. My nightmare was over. He said I had been in here for seven months. It seemed like seven years. It couldn't end too soon. I took a seat across the table from my sweaty Aussie saviour. A pudgy guard eyed us from the hut's corner.

"I'm really glad to see you," I said.

"Me, too. The Canadian officials in Bangkok have been ringing me hourly. You're causing quite a stir back in Canada."

"Really?"

"Yeah, your mom won't rest. I think she's contacted every newspaper, radio station, and magazine in your country."

I swallowed. I thought about how much I wanted to see her.

"Why hasn't she come again?"

"Son, believe me, she's trying. She's at the prison gates every day trying to convince them to let her in. They're afraid she'll talk too much to the international press."

"How about Somchai?"

"Ah, yes, your friend. He was roughed up, but he's okay. They haven't come for him again. His mother won't let him anywhere near this place. She's afraid they'll lock him up, too."

"But he hasn't done anything wrong."

"Have you?"

"No," I said quickly. Maybe too quickly. The truth was I had done so many things wrong. Maybe I had even caused Nok's death. If I had been at that party she could still be alive today. My anger had gotten in the way of my whole life.

After some silence Ned Jones looked away and shuffled through some papers.

"So when am I getting out?"

He looked up from his papers with a look of surprise on his leathery face. He scratched the back of his neck.

"Getting out? You need to have a trial first."

I sucked in a clipped inhale. I forced myself to try to breathe. Really breathe. All the way down into my belly, like Sai taught me. But my chest tightened.

"When is that going to be?" I asked, breathless.

"We're putting the pressure on, Cam. I assure you. A Canadian officer from the embassy in Bangkok is making plans to come here and meet with some government folks. They've got a lawyer to work on your case. We're making steps."

"Mr. Jones, I can't stay here anymore. I can't."

He reached across the table to lay a hand on my shoulder. I brushed it off. The guard placed a hand on the pistol hanging from his hip.

"Cam, we are doing everything we can."

The guard coughed and pointed to the clock.

"I'm sorry, but I need to go now. I'll see you next month."

"Next month? What the fuck? You can't leave me here."

"Cam, you have to understand. We have to respect the rules of the country."

The guard opened the door, flooding the dim room with severe sunlight. Mr. Jones straightened his pile of papers and tucked them into his briefcase. He was nothing but a dark shadow as he paused briefly in the doorframe, the bright sun of freedom behind him.

POLITICAL RE-EDUCATION

Seng

Vong bought some incense from the corner store near the guesthouse.

"I want to burn it for Nok at the spirit house in front of where we're staying," she told Seng. She seemed edgier today, talking more quickly, her movements more abrupt. He worried that her money was running out. He said he would come, too.

The guesthouse courtyard was overflowing with red hibiscus bushes, birds of paradise, and leafy banana plants. A little pool was in the centre with orange and white koi swimming around. In a far corner sat the little spirit house on a rough wooden post. After mouthing their prayers, they sat for a long time on a grey, stone bench underneath an ancient banyan tree. There was nothing else to do. Nowhere else to go. They were drifting — without a home or a purpose. Seven whole months had passed and they still had no plan. They were only living off Vong's savings.

The incense smoke crawled lazily up from the spirit house before vanishing into the smoggy sky. Vong rubbed the top of her thighs over and over again. He listened to the swishing sound her hands made as they ran along her polyester pants.

"Vong? Do you think Pa and Meh could still be alive?"
She turned to face him.

"Don't be ridiculous, Seng."

"Did Meh have any sisters who looked like her?"

"No. Don't you think we would have known our aunts?"

"How did we find out that they died?"

"A letter from the government."

"Did we get their ashes?"

"We got Pa's, but not Meh's. Seng, why are you asking me all of this stuff?"

"I just miss her, that's all."

He looked down into his hands in his lap. Of course the spring-roll woman couldn't be their mom. She would have recognized her son. This whole situation was just making him crazy.

MEH

Seng

There was nothing to do while Seng and Vong struggled to come up with a plan. But the next day, he was drawn back to Khaosan Road like a magnet. He sat on the stoop of the boarded-up shop where he had sat before, watching his spring-roll woman. He thought she kept peering over in his direction. Finally, when she had a break in between customers, she feebly walked toward him. His heart beat faster.

"You are not with the police?" she asked, standing taller.

"Definitely not," he said.

"I know who you are, then."

She slipped him a piece of paper. It was a crumpled flyer from one of the massage houses, damp with sweat. He took it and thought a smile might have passed briefly over her thin lips. She glanced nervously all around before picking up her basket and disappearing into the crowd on the sidewalk. With trembling hands he turned the flyer over and read what she had written on the other side.

"Wait!" he screamed.

He ran after her, snaking his way through the Khao-san crowd.

"Wait!"

He finally spotted her getting on a busy bus. He stood on the sidewalk and watched, tears like rivers down his cheeks, as the bus pulled away. His mother watched him from the window. He read the note again.

> *Emkhan Mannivong*
> *Apartment 8*
> *Savoy Apartments*
> *Suhnthon Kosa Road*

THE MIDDLE WAY

Cam

I sat with Sai in meditation every day. Early each morning, before the guards came to get us for work.

"You two lose your mind," Huang said, watching us and laughing.

"No, we're watching our minds," Sai said.

I couldn't believe how my mind flipped all the time between the past and the future. I hardly ever thought about what was real, what was happening at that very exact moment. I rarely noticed the present.

"It's normal," Sai said. "You can't stop your mind from thinking. That's what it was made to do. Just watch it, like you were sitting on a riverbank, watching your thoughts float by. Observe each thought and then let it go, don't add on to it or follow it. It's how you can control your mind instead of it controlling you. When you notice your mind wandering just bring your attention back to your breath. It's your link to what is true right now."

When I'd sat like that long enough I would start to feel

kind of tingly and high. Suddenly I would feel bigger than myself. I would see how so much of my anger came from my childhood. When I breathed long enough I could let it go. I felt so light.

"Crazy, crazy." Huang clicked his tongue.

That day I was put to work digging another pond to house more catfish. It was how the guards supplemented their income. I don't think they made much money being guards. I was working with three other guys, none of them from my cell. One was Eastern European and didn't speak English. The other two were Vietnamese. One of them had some English; he said his name was Trahn. The work was backbreaking. We thrust rusty shovels into the ground over and over again. The muscles between my shoulder blades began to spasm. Suddenly Trahn's friend collapsed. I dropped my shovel and ran to him.

He was lying on his back, his arms stretched out by his sides, eyes fluttering. "What's wrong with him?" I asked Trahn. The guy was panicking, shaking his friend's shoulders.

"He not eat in a week. He's very weak. He never gets broth or rice. The big guy in our cell eats most."

A guard blew a whistle and came running over to us.

"Back to work," he barked. He started to push Trahn off his friend. We walked reluctantly back to our shovels. The collapsed man lay limp on the dirt. The guard kicked him in the leg and then turned to walk away, glancing over his shoulder at us every now and then. When he rounded the corner I crept back to Trahn.

"I'll be back," I whispered.

"You'll be in big trouble!" he said. "Interrogation room!"

I glanced all around to make sure no one was watching.

Then I walked swiftly to the guards' staff room. None of them would be there yet. It was too early for their break. Looking over my shoulder, I turned to slowly open the door. It creaked noisily on its hinges. My fearful heart beat deafeningly inside my ribcage. I quickly scanned the room and saw a huge bottle of water sitting on a water tipper. I picked a metal cup off the counter and quickly tipped the huge bottle to fill the cup with water. I was too hasty and some water sloshed on the floor. I turned to walk as quickly as I could out of the room without spilling the water. Trahn looked at me with awe as I approached. I bent over his friend and trickled water through the thin parting of his lips. My hands were shaking and I spilled some on the man's chest. His eyes fluttered and he began to swallow.

"Now I'll get you food," I whispered in his ear.

"Thank you," Trahn whispered to me. "Your heart so kind. But you need to stop. You get us all in trouble."

I couldn't stop. I was eighteen and had never thought beyond what I wanted or how sorry I was for myself. Suddenly serving this weak man was giving me power. For once I felt purposeful. Destined. I suddenly realized how helping him would save me.

I took the empty cup with me so the guys wouldn't get in trouble if a guard came while I was gone. I skulked to the stinking room where the fish were cleaned. I saw a prisoner bent over the pile of fish corpses, gutting them with a knife. A bored-looking guard watched him inattentively from the corner. I was nauseous, but something urged me on. I didn't want the other prisoner to see me, otherwise he'd be implicated, too. I waited and watched until the guard left, likely to take a piss. The prisoner gutted another fish and then stood to stretch. He turned his back to me as he twisted his body from side to side, trying to get the kinks out of his hunched back. It was my moment. I swallowed. I slunk into the room, grabbed two slippery catfish, and was gone.

I sped-walked back to the site where we were digging the pond. I had a fish tucked under each armpit. I surreptitiously passed them to Trahn, who was helping his weak friend sit up.

"Here. Feed these to him. I can get you more later," I whispered. I resolved to find a way to bring my share of the catfish to Trahn's cell.

"But, the guard, he —" Trahn was interrupted as the guard who had kicked his friend came running across the field to us.

"You!" He pointed at me. "I was here two minutes ago and you weren't. Where were you?"

I saw the grim expression on Trahn's face.

"Answer!" the guard barked.

"Getting food," I said. "He will die without it." I pointed to the prisoner sitting on the ground and looking around, dazed.

"He gets food," the guard spat.

"Not enough."

"I didn't want to do this, but you could have got me in big trouble. I've had to report you to my supervisor," the guard said. "Tomorrow you'll have a meeting with him. He said he'd take you to the interrogation room himself."

I heard Trahn's shovel drop.

MEMORY

Seng

The next morning Vong found the wrinkled piece of paper with Meh's address lying on the bedside table of their guesthouse room.

"What's this?" she asked.

For once he knew something that she didn't. For once he was in control. He had taken life into his own hands. He paused to savour the feeling for a moment. He considered not telling her. She read their mother's stout characters, scratched out in a weak pen that looked like it was almost out of ink.

"Seng?"

"She's alive, Vong." He met her eyes. "Meh."

Vong flopped down in the wooden guesthouse chair.

"What are you saying?"

"I found her." *He* found her. No one else. He started to laugh. He had done the very thing he had dreamed of his entire life. By himself.

"Our mom is alive, *euaigh*!" He reached down and hugged his sister. "She's here, in Bangkok." He laughed hysterically. He buried his face into his sister's shoulder and his wild laughter gradually changed into wild sobbing. They sat for a long time, Seng laughing and weeping, Vong with a confused look on her face.

"I can't wait anymore. We will go see her today," Seng said, when they finally calmed down.

"We will see our mother today?" Vong asked, eyes wide. "I don't believe this. You must have it all wrong. Is it the stress? Tell me everything."

"Let's go! I've been waiting to see her since I was five years old. I can't wait any longer," he said.

Outside the guesthouse, Seng reluctantly handed the flyer over to a *tuk-tuk* driver. He was afraid to let it go, his only link to his mom. The driver nodded and Seng immediately took the flyer and put it into the pocket over his heart.

The driver let them off in front of a grey, brick tenement. Faded skirts with patterns of elephants and men's white undershirts flapped from laundry lines strung across balconies that were overflowing with stuff — boisterous chickens in cages, bicycles, and tattered wicker baskets. Barefoot children in dirty, worn clothes chased each other outside. The smell of smouldering garbage fires was everywhere.

Vong and Seng stepped over a beggar sitting on the cement steps. It looked like she lived in the stairwell. A cardboard box had been laid out flat underneath the stairs. A child sat on it, absent-mindedly forming grains of rice into a picture. She wore no top and her light brown hair frizzed around her head. Vong pressed a few *baht* into the woman's lined, brown palm.

"Please, miss. Can you tell us where apartment number 8 is?" Vong's voice was shaky.

They followed the young woman's directions to the top of the grimy stairs and made a left into a dim, grey hall. With quivering hands, Seng knocked on the door. No one answered. Outside children called out to each other. A coin fell out of his pocket and tingled loudly on the dirty linoleum floor.

"Are you sure it was her, Seng?" Vong asked.

This time they could hear shuffling behind the thin door. The unlatching of locks. The creaking of hinges. And suddenly there she was. For the first time Seng saw her without her dark sunglasses.

Of course.

His mother.

Eyes exactly like his own stared back at him. The smell of frying spring rolls wafted out from behind her.

"Meh!" Seng fell at her feet. "Meh!" He began to weep. Vong wiped her eyes.

"Mother, it's us. Vong and Seng."

A ghost of a smile passed over their mother's cracked lips.

A door creaking open across the hallway interrupted the moment.

"Mrs. Emkhan. Everything okay?" asked a toothless, young woman.

"Yes, yes. Just the man looking for rent again," their mother spoke.

Vong shot Seng a confused look.

"Okay, Missus." The woman turned to speak to Vong and Seng. "I always check up on her, you know. She doesn't remember stuff. Something wrong with her head."

Seng didn't believe the woman. After all, Meh had remembered him. The woman looked Seng and Vong up and down and seemed to decide they weren't a threat. She went back into her apartment, shutting the scratched, blue door behind her.

"May we come in, Meh?" Seng finally said.

"Yes, yes, of course, although I already paid my rent." Their mother stepped to the side so Vong and Seng could enter.

Was this act so the neighbours wouldn't know?

The small apartment was cluttered with papers, bags of rice, and pots and pans. There was stuff everywhere. A rice cooker in the bathroom. Crumpled newspapers on the floor. Weak sunlight snuck in through a small, smudged window. On an overflowing bookcase made from cinder blocks and planks of wood Vong spotted a book with a Lao title.

"Vong!" Seng whispered and pointed at a tattered black-and-white photograph stuck to the wall with masking tape. It was of the three of them as children. Nok was squinting in the sun at the camera. Seng's throat caught.

"Meh." Seng went into the kitchen where their mom was using tongs to take spring rolls out of a pot of boiling oil. He wanted to hold her hands, hug her, but instead Meh put the food on a plate and placed it on the floor. The three sat around the plate and ate silently. There was too much to say.

"Not too many because I have to sell them today. And I already paid you rent, I said."

"Meh, you can stop the charade now. It's me," Seng tried again. Emkhan looked up at him with blank eyes. She began to wring her hands. "Remember — we found each other on Khaosan Road?"

She began to rock back and forth on her knees.

"Seng, what's going on?" Vong asked.

"I don't know. She remembered me. She gave me her address. Now it's as if she doesn't know us." He swallowed the lump in his throat.

"Meh, do you remember this? How you would wave to me every morning from our driveway? When I was five. I would get on my bike and you would stand there until we couldn't see each other anymore. Every morning you did that. Every single morning." His voice was beginning to sound frantic and cheery in a forced way.

"And do you remember how Nok, just a baby, would try to massage your feet after dinner? Her hands were so small but she was trying to copy Vong. Do you remember that? Meh?" He chuckled awkwardly. Meh began to tear up a tissue she was holding in her hand.

Vong reached over to lay one hand on top of her mother's. Emkhan brushed it aside.

"What about when we would walk past the grounds of the king's palace and you would make up funny stories about how the dragon statues came to be sitting on the temple steps?" His volume was rising with intensity. "Do you remember, Meh?"

"I don't know why you came here. I paid you the rent. I pay every month on time. You should leave an old woman alone."

He slapped his palm against the insubstantial apartment wall.

The toothless woman from across the hall creaked Meh's door open.

"Mrs. Emhkan, what's going on?" she asked, a look of concern on her face.

"Is something wrong with her?" Vong asked.

"Yes, I told you. She doesn't remember a lot of the time. I think it's called Alzheimer's. Sometimes she remembers and her mind is clear as anything, but then it goes again. I look out for her. She used to help me when she was well. Watch my kids and stuff."

Seng hung his head and began to sob noisily. This was everything he had ever dreamed of. It had come to him like an unexpected gift only to be cruelly snatched away before he could open it. Vong stood up and went to place a hand on his shoulder while their mother rocked back and forth.

"I know you're not here for the rent because we have the same landlord," the woman said. "So who are you?"

"Her children," Vong said. Seng couldn't speak.

"Oh!" the woman raised a hand to her mouth. "Finally."

"She told you about us?" Vong asked.

"Yes, yes. One day she kept calling me Nok. She showed me this." She walked over to the makeshift bookshelf and pulled out a book. Tucked inside was a yellowing envelope.

"Here, take it," the woman said. It had their address in Vientiane written on it. Meh had known where they lived?

"You're Nok?" the woman asked Vong.

"No, her older sister," Vong said, and looked to her feet.

Seng opened the envelope.

DEATH PENALTY

Cam

"I hear you yell at Sai last week," Huang said to me one morning. His hot, putrid morning breath met my nose. "Huang tell you he no better."

"No, you're wrong," I said. "Sai's not like that."

"You give me Sai's fish, I give you blanket."

"Never."

"You know nothing about world." Huang shook his head.

I ignored him and turned to get dressed. I didn't have time for Huang. My mind was racing about the interrogation room. There were stories of mock executions that left prisoners so shaken they couldn't walk back to their cells. Beatings that broke prisoners' teeth. My body shivered with cold perspiration.

"I hear you in jail for manslaughter," Huang said.

I felt my throat go dry. How did he know?

"You kill girlfriend. Lao girl." Huang looked at me from his one good eye. "You in big, big trouble." He wagged a finger at me. I could see its freakishly long, yellow nail.

I began to breathe long and slow. I stood taller. I wouldn't answer. I wouldn't react.

Huang leaned in closer.

"You know in Laos they execute for manslaughter?"

"What?"

"No one want to tell you. They not want to worry you. Your punishment will be death penalty. I hear guards talking."

I felt my breath go shallow. I froze.

"You don't know what you're talking about, Huang. You're just trying to scare me into giving you fish."

"They execute Nigerian man last year. You don't believe Huang, you ask Sai, you love him so much." Huang's chuckle was menacing. "You not alive for long, no matter how much fish you eat."

I couldn't think. My mind was racing every which way. How did Huang know about the manslaughter charges? He must have overheard something. And I had overheard some of the guys talking about the Nigerian man who was executed. I needed to talk to Sai.

I chewed my fingernails. My palms were damp. I hadn't even met my lawyer yet. I couldn't wait for legal stuff. I had to get out on my own. I heard the cell door clanking open and jumped. But it was just Sai being guided back into the cell. I went up to him.

"Can we talk?" I whispered.

"Yeah, you ask him. He tell you!" Huang called out from his shadowy corner.

"Sai," I pulled him by the arm around the corner into the bathroom so no one could hear us.

"What's going on, friend?" he asked.

"In Laos do they give the death penalty for manslaughter?"

Sai's face froze momentarily. "Yes," he answered.

I could tell by the way he answered that he knew what the charges were against me. He knew I was here for more than a basketball fight.

"You've known all along, haven't you? About the charges against me."

Sai nodded.

And still he had befriended me.

"Sai, are they going to execute me? Am I going to die here?" I stood, aghast.

"Cam, you know how hard your mom is working to get you out. Stay focused on what is real right now, not on your fears."

He didn't say no. He didn't say *Cam, don't be ridiculous.*

"I know what is real. They're going to take me to the interrogation room any minute now." I told Sai about the Vietnamese prisoner who had collapsed from hunger.

"Cam." Sai looked at me deeply. "Your heart has grown."

"Yes, but Sai," I said, "will you help me escape?"

THE CHOICE

Seng

The silence in their guesthouse room was charged. Seng had scarcely said two words since their visit with their mom. First he had lost his sister and now he had lost his mother — for the second time. He wondered how much one person could stand. He would give anything to have his simple life in Vientiane back. Pedalling home to find Nok sifting rice for dinner, sitting on the riverbank with Khamdeng with his dreams of a better life in America. Now his dreams consisted of him lying on top of a funeral pyre, thick smoke suffocating him, flames licking at his thighs, the sound of sizzling flesh.

"We should talk about what we're going to do next," Vong's voice broke his thoughts. "Meh can't live by herself like that."

Seng nodded, but said nothing.

"We're nearly out of money," Vong continued. "I don't know what we can do. I think I should call Chit and tell him everything."

Seng thought about how strange it was that he had only met his brother-in-law once, when he had come to Vientiane and taken Vong away from them.

"I've been putting off explaining things to him. I don't want him to worry, or become mixed up in this mess I've created," Vong continued.

"*You've* created?"

"It was my plan."

"Yeah, but it was my crime. And I'm the one who found Meh." *You can't take that away from me*, he thought.

"I should have never left you and Nok in the first place. I tricked myself into thinking everything was okay here. I'm really sorry, brother. For leaving."

"I'll come with you to call Chit."

They walked together to the payphone on the corner. Seng stood just in front of the booth. He watched as she dialled. He could only hear Vong's side of the conversation.

"I'm sorry I haven't called. It's been busy, and you know how expensive it is to call from Laos. You got my e-mails, though."

She had a guilty look on her face.

"You mean the accident is on the news there? Nok's? But why? It happened months ago."

There was silence as Chit filled in the blanks. Seng still hadn't mentioned the Canadian boyfriend to Vong.

Vong ran her index finger along the hard edges of the payphone. She eyed her fingernails, nearly chewed to the quick. She wouldn't make eye contact with him. He wondered what she knew now. He kicked a stone on the ground.

"Well, I knew she had a Canadian boyfriend but —"

She hung her head.

"Yes, I'm here," she finally said in a small voice. "He's in jail?"

Seng froze. He raised his hands to his head. In jail? They had actually jailed a foreigner. For his crime.

Vong opened her mouth to speak, but couldn't. A motorbike revved its engine behind her.

"Chit, I'm not in Laos," she suddenly blurted out.

She told him everything. Seng's crime. The escape. Hiding out in Thailand. Finding their mother. She talked so quickly Seng wondered how Chit could understand. Seng glanced around to make sure no one was in earshot. They were getting sloppy with their hiding.

Now there was nothing but silence coming from the phone booth. Minutes ticked away. Seng felt panic racing through his veins. Vong twisted the phone cord around and around. She wouldn't look at him.

"I don't know what to do next." She leaned her forehead on the top of the phone. Then she began to gently bang her forehead on it, over and over.

She switched sides.

"What do you mean — they make deals?"

A truck blared its horn.

She suddenly stood tall and listened for a long time.

"Never," she finally said. Then she slammed the phone down violently. She turned and ran. Weaving in and out of the packed sidewalks, down onto the street, and nearly into a car. The driver blared the horn angrily at her.

Seng followed. When he caught up to her she was bent over, clutching her middle, and breathing heavily. He laid a hand on her back.

"How come you didn't tell me about the Canadian?" she screamed, looking up at him.

"Shame," Seng said quietly.

"He's in jail, Seng." She wiped her eyes with the back of her hand.

"Jail? But I thought they took it easy on foreigners."

"Seng, how can you be so fucking clueless about the world?" She brushed his hand off her back.

Seng was stunned. Her anger cut him like a knife.

"Don't talk to me like I'm an idiot, Vong. I haven't been outside of Laos like you have. Remember, you left us behind."

She didn't answer.

"We have to get the Canadian out of jail," he finally said.

"That means you'll take his place," she said. "Do you know what they'll do to you in jail? You fled the scene of the crime. You killed your own sister!"

Seng hung his head and buried his face in his hands.

She stood up and took a deep breath. "I'm sorry, Seng. I shouldn't have said that."

"It's true," he said.

Vong looked at the ground, hands on hips, panting.

"What did Chit say?" he asked.

"I can't even say it. His idea. It's awful." She pressed her lips together until they turned white.

"We need all the ideas we can get."

"No we don't. We don't need this one."

Seng looked away.

Vong sighed. "Chit said Meh's only going to get worse." She looked down at the ground. "At least he's right about that. It won't be long before she doesn't even know where she is."

Seng nodded sadly.

"He thinks as long as someone brings her food and pays for her medicine, she would be okay."

"But we can't leave her alone in her apartment."

"That's not what he's talking about."

Seng looked Vong straight in the eyes. "A Royal Lao government employee who successfully escaped from re-education camp so many years ago. In prison. Chit says it would send a strong message. The communists would like it."

"What does he mean?"

"Turning Meh in. In exchange for your freedom."

"He can't be serious." It was as if Vong had started to speak another language. He couldn't understand her.

"He is. He says if we go back to Laos, your life is on the line. You've heard about Lao prisons. But they'd go easy on an elderly woman. Especially one with Alzheimer's."

"He really thinks I'd send my mother to jail?" he asked. "What kind of person is he?"

"He's just trying to save your life, Seng. Meh wouldn't even know. She would be fed, have shelter. And you would be free. If Meh could make the choice, she would do it, I know she would. You read her letter. She was desperate to contact us all of these years, but she knew it would put us in danger. She wouldn't want your freedom taken from you like hers was." Her words were suddenly calm and measured.

"You agree with him?" Seng asked, an unfamiliar rage filling his heart.

"Forget I even said it. I just —"

"What?" he stopped.

"I don't want to fail you again. Neglect you. I'm just trying to figure things out."

"You don't need to, Vong. I don't need you to. I will find my way."

THE WAY

Seng

The silence in the guestroom was still overbearing. Seng had barely spoken to Vong since she'd put the awful choice in front of him two days ago. He and the Canadian could be free if they'd only turn in Meh. He didn't want to think about it. He tried to figure out how to use the remote control for the guesthouse TV and he learned how to dial the phone to order in food. He didn't even bother to defer to Vong anymore, as he usually would have. *Euaigh, what should we eat for dinner?*

"Stop," she said the next morning, as he picked up the phone. He put the old, rotary dial phone back on its hook and looked at her. "We don't have any more money," she said flatly.

He sat silently on the yellow guesthouse bedspread for a long time. He flicked through the channels on the TV. The police sirens from a television drama pierced the room. He clicked it off.

"I could sell some stuff," he finally said. "Like I do in Vientiane."

"We don't have anything to sell."

He looked around the room. "You have that backpack. Some things from Canada."

"Who's going to buy my old, worn stuff?"

"You'd be surprised."

But he wasn't even convincing himself. He felt light-headed.

"Can't Chit send us some cash?"

"Maybe, but then I'd have to give the bank my name. You have to show identification to pick up wired money."

Seng flipped the remote over and over in his hand. Finally Vong said she was going out.

"Where?" he asked.

"I need some fresh air," she said.

She never went out for fresh air anymore. She thought it was too risky. Morning slowly gave way to afternoon as Seng waited. He started to imagine that someone had spotted her on the street and turned her in, or she had become mixed up in the countless dangerous ways people make money in this swarming city so they can survive. The hunger gnawed on the sides of his stomach, but he stopped noticing. To lift up even one heavy arm seemed like a chore.

Through the thin guesthouse wall he could hear a TV in the room beside him. He heard a car revving its engine outside the window. Smelled fried rice being prepared in someone's kitchen. Heard the shrill call of a police siren. A cool November breeze seeped in through the window and he shivered.

By the time she came back, the room was black with night and Seng could see white starbursts whenever he closed his eyes. He had never been so hungry. He was actually glad for the faint, fuzzy feeling in his head. It was helping him keep his mind off Meh and the Canadian.

"Let's go see Meh tomorrow," Vong said.

Seng was so lethargic from hunger that he just nodded.

The next morning they locked the wooden guesthouse door with a clunky key. Their footsteps echoed as they walked down the empty hall. All of the guests would be out, touring the ornate grounds of the Royal Palace or laying on mattresses to get massages at Wat Po. They were going out to see the mother they had lost so many years ago, to watch her slip through their hands once more.

They found themselves at a crowded bus stop, where the thick smell of diesel met Seng's nose.

"Shouldn't we walk?" Seng asked. "We don't have any money."

"I found a few *baht* in a pocket in my backpack," Vong said.

He watched families from the grimy window. A young mother held her toddler's hand. A family of four jammed onto one singular motorbike. A man gently held an elderly gentlemen's elbow as they navigated their way through the teeming streets.

They got off in front of their mother's apartment building. The beggar and her young daughter recognized them.

"Apartment 8 up there," the poor woman said.

"Thanks."

Seng stopped and met the beggar's eyes, soft brown and watery. Vong reached in her purse, she said she was looking for a *kanom* she had bought to snack on a couple days before and passed it to the poor woman. Vong had snacks in her purse?

The woman inspected the cake wrapped in clear plastic, held it up to her nose, and sniffed, and passed it to her daughter. The little girl hastily tore the package open and chewed hungrily.

"You must be hungry, too," Seng said to the woman.

"Children first."

"Of course," Seng said. Motherhood before hunger.

They climbed the grey, dusty staircase to the eighth floor. Maybe Meh would be having one of her clear moments. He would find a way to make it better for her, for all of them. He knocked on the blue door, but there was no answer. He knocked a bit louder. He turned to look at Vong, but she looked down the hall uncomfortably. He placed his ear against it, but couldn't hear any noise inside. From behind him he heard a door creaking on its hinges. It was the toothless woman from across the hallway.

"She's not here," the woman said. "She said she was going home. A man came and helped her pack up her things. He said he would make sure she got back to her country safely."

"Back to Laos? What man?" Seng's heart was racing. He looked back and forth between Vong and the woman. "What's going on?"

"He looked Lao or Thai, but he could only speak English," the woman explained. "I didn't understand much of what he said."

"Vong, what's going on?" Seng demanded.

"Chit," she said in a small voice. "It was Chit." Then she fell onto her knees in the hallway and wept.

Seng turned and ran as fast he could.

230

MERIT

Cam

"Take all of your things," the guard with the missing front tooth said.

I looked at him, confused. Why did I need to take all of my things? Wouldn't I come back from the interrogation room?

"*Muht!* Everything."

I turned around to look at Sai. He made his breath loud and audible. He was breathing for me. I could barely get an inhale.

I shoved the little bit of stuff I had under one arm — a toothbrush; a bar of soap; the thin, Thai farmer pants I wore to sleep. The guard clutched me by the other arm and led me down the hallway. My throat thickened as I wondered what they would do to me. I remembered the blood-curdling screams coming from the interrogation room. Whatever they did, they would never be able to take away the day I had helped the collapsed prisoner. On that day I had undone my own cage, found my own victory.

The guard led me past the fish ponds and in between the garden hedges. When we marched past the visitor's hut my heart began to thunder so hard I thought it might break my ribs. I could see the interrogation hut now. I tried not to think about the guards waiting there for me. The ones instructed to conduct the torture. From my peripheral vision I noticed the empty guard tower on the east corner of the compound. For some reason that one was rarely manned, just like Sai had said. I scanned the guard roughly dragging me along. I was bigger than him, but I was weak from my months in prison. Still, I thought I could take him. The compound was post-lunch quiet. I spotted one guard dozing on the veranda. This was my chance. I eyed the guard's pistol dangling from his hip. It didn't seem to be fastened to anything — just tucked carelessly into his pocket. If I moved quickly enough I could grab it.

The prison's main gate wasn't far from the interrogation room. I would wait until we were there to make my move. It was risky, in broad daylight and everything, but I didn't have another option. I wasn't stepping foot in the interrogation room. I would rather die. I heard a rooster cackling from the vegetable garden. I would pretend to stumble and knock the guard's gun from its holster. I was bigger, I'd be able to handle him. No one else seemed to be around.

But something stopped me dead in my tracks.

Something moved in my peripheral vision — something waving and white, like a flag of surrender.

I turned to look.

It was Mom.

She was waving wildly from the red prison gate and beaming from ear to ear. I suddenly realized that the guard was leading me toward her! I began to quicken my pace.

Soon I was running. The guard, in a flash of compassion, jogged along beside me. I think he was smiling.

Mom was sobbing. The guard fiddled with a ring of keys at his hip. The door clanged as he slid it open and released me.

Before I knew it I was standing in front of my mom with nothing between us — no bars, and no resentment. Nothing but the moment existed. She clutched me to her heaving chest. "The driver of the bike. It was Nok's brother. He turned himself in. You're free, Cam. The charges have been dropped. You're free!"

Seng.

I remembered Nok saying his name.

I dropped to my knees. My mom encircled me, my hair growing damp with her tears. I was free — in more ways than one.

SHINE

Seng

Every day she comes. She brings a basket of sticky rice, some spring rolls, a little bit of *padek*. She arrives at his cell door, shoulders rounded, eyes not understanding why she is here or how she came to be at this place. She doesn't seem to know that it is her son she serves every day. The guards think she is just a spring-roll lady from downtown Vientiane trying to build her merit.

After a guard opens the cell door and she slides the food toward Seng across the dank, cement floor, she pauses. She stares at her son. A bewildered, puzzled look on her face. But underneath the fog, behind the confusion, there is something in her eyes.

Seng thinks it is love.

Somehow it persists.

Through sickness and fear, through judgment and years, it shines, despite everything.

SAI'S ONE-MINUTE BREATH

The One-Minute Breath instructions provided in this book have been reviewed and approved by the Kundalini Research Institute (KRI).

This breath pattern, taught to Cam in jail by Sai, was originally taught by Yogi Bhajan, Master of Kundalini Yoga. It calms anxiety, fear and worry. Ask your health-care practitioner if it's right for you.

For each count of 20, begin with a count of 8 seconds. As your lung capacity builds, you can slowly work your way up to a count of 20.

❧

Inhale through the nostrils for 20 seconds.
Hold the breath for 20 seconds.
Try to relax around the suspended breath. Don't tighten your face or other muscles.
Exhale through the nostrils for 20 seconds.
Repeat for 5 minutes.
For powerful results practice every day.

❧

For more information consult an instructor of Kundalini Yoga as taught by Yogi Bhajan® in your area.

ACKNOWLEDGEMENTS

I am grateful to the people of Laos and what they have taught me with their open hearts and dedication to what truly matters in life. I am also thankful to Yogi Bhajan, master of Kundalini Yoga, who risked his life to bring teachings like the One-Minute Breath to us.

Thanks to my editor, Shannon Whibbs, and all of the people at Dundurn who have worked on this book. It would not be in your hands without Sylvia McConnell, who believed in it enough to take it against great odds. Thanks to my teacher, Sharelle Byars Moranville, whose comments helped me see the forest for the trees and to Rick Taylor, who has been generous with his time and help.

I would like to thank my first readers, who bravely agreed to comment on early drafts: Jean-Philippe Veilleux, Cole Powell, Bethany Powell Archambault, Imran Arshad, Bert Powell, Paula Powell, Roger Mollot, and Zoë Boutilier. I'm grateful to Gwen Frankton for her creativity and generosity.

Thanks to my parents, who have enthusiastically read everything I've ever written, and to my daughter, who at ten years old is better at promoting my work than myself. Gratitude also goes to my two sons, who were the inspiration for the love between mothers and sons that I attempted to explore in this book.

Finally, thank you to Imran, whose love, support, and belief in me makes impossible things possible.